A GOOD TIME
IN THE HOOD

First Edition

Published by The Nazca Plains Corporation
Las Vegas, Nevada
2010

ISBN: 978-1-935509-73-8

Published by

The Nazca Plains Corporation ®
4640 Paradise Rd, Suite 141
Las Vegas NV 89109-8000

PUBLISHER'S NOTE
A Good Time in the Hood is a work of fiction created wholly by *Diesel King's* imagination. All characters are fictional and any resemblance to any persons living or deceased is purely by accident. No portion of this book reflects any real person or events.

Cover, Santiago
Art Director, Blake Stephens

DEDICATION

for all those
that have
graciously fallen to their knees
before me

A GOOD TIME IN THE HOOD

First Edition

Diesel King

CONTENTS

Introduction   1

A Good Time in the Hood   7

Hours after the Bar Closes   21

Bangers   51

Worked Loose   61

Married to the Game   79

48 & 50   87

Chat Room   139

Young Buck   159

Exit Interview   169

About the Author   187

INTRODUCTION

C'mon in! Lay back, relax, and let me show you a kick-ass good time!

Isn't that what it's really all about? Isn't that what the cover of most of these homoerotic books suggests? Isn't that what you expect after sinking in your hard-earned money into getting aroused? Isn't that what you, at a minimum, deserve to get?

I know, I know, and I am totally fucking feel you! The exact same thing has been promised before, many times many ways, by the countless motherfuckers that have composed other short story collections. In my own experience, be it one author or an anthology of diverse authors, there have only been a select few that even bothered to step up to the plate and hit a homerun, rising to the rare occasion of coming close to being mildly satisfying. Most, however, have fallen by the waist side of great expectations, promising exotic travels of the seven continents and four oceans in the front just to come around the back with some lame-ass pocket-size black-and-white map of the world. Not even making an effort to add some color to the fray or putting it on a life-like globe. If lucky—only if so fucking lucky—coming across a collection that can muster up one or two good stories worth flipping through as an alternative to flipping on the porn out there.

As you can probably tell, I've been there, too.

Too many times to count and too many times to even want to remember!

Lured in by some muscled-up masculine fuck on the cover ready to have the best time a swinging greased dick and a large calloused mitt can offer, just for the storyline to leave me hanging for the mechanics of mundane sex like a steady cocktease that has absolutely no intention of cleaning up the sloppy mess they left behind.

If you think you got it bad, it's a double whammy for me.

Don't even get me started on those Black or Latin or any other specifically-themed ethnic titles, both in literary and visual forms. As a strong, (like to think) easy-on-the-eyes, tall, husky, muscled-up, very well hung and uncut, leather-lovin' shaven head cuttin', no doubt tatted up and pierced down no-hold barred black man from the wrong sides of the tracks, I have just about abandoned them all. Why? It is almost always a certified guaranteed disappointment. Not always, but most times. So I hold on tight to the few gems that are out there and are still being produced, in spite of the bureaucratic rigmaroles. Just as sure as a positive DNA test, I am bound to run up against a fortified wall of watered down versions of the erotic adventures of so-called men of color, hosted by the anorexic runts of the pack and chronicled by the none-threatening array of flaming sissies masked in war paint and rogue. And if that isn't enough, throwing in some token white boy wanting to either live out his Mandingo fantasy or try and "diversify" the reading audience. I don't know about you, but when I fuck a white boy it is solely for my pleasure over playing into his taboo OMG big black dick fantasy. If it happens to be one in the same, if he gets that in, then it is still all good in having a good time.

Even with all that being said, it doesn't mean I have given up entire on finding that title that can make me stand up while sitting down.

Far from it.

Flipping through the pages of some of these kinds of books, my engine gets easily revved up by the cover alone, despite of my previous histories. And if I am fortunate for it to read right, I know it'll let me down quite satisfied after playing into my own deepest, darkest, and depraved fantasies.

It is what I expect. It is what I think I deserve. Don't you?

The next question that comes into mind, if you're a deep post-ejaculating thinker like myself is, is it all fantasy or is it all real? Is any of it real? Or does it hold just enough slither of truth, twisted and turned just to come off as something that genuinely happened?

Everyone tries to sound authentic, name-dropping certain landmarks of gay men and rough trade from San Francisco and New York, to add to their street cred. While I too have peed on some trees in many of these same exact places, from Castro Street to Christopher Street, I have also had a good time in the many places in between, without the safety net of those "safe spaces."

I've had a good time getting blown off on a rural bike trail in Colorado. I've had a good time turning out this Mormon kid straight off the compound. I've had a good time showing innocent farm hands how to handle an honest to goodness real cowpoke in the corn and wheat fields of the Midwest. I've had a good time with this hairy butch down in the Deep South, forcing him to parade around in women's panties and making him the "house bitch" for a room full of horny big-dick poker studs. I've had a good time drenching this big-time drug dealer out in Syracuse in a golden shower, washing away his many sins against my community. I've had a good time engaging in a beachside orgy on the Dark Continent; banging cock in Thailand. I've even had a good time cruising local parks and by simply making a bootycall on a fellow neighbor across the way that turned into something that I wasn't expecting, with a strong emphasis that in every situation I had a *really* good time.

But the best time I ever had was right in the neighborhood, regardless of where I lived or traveled at the time, either right here at the house or a few blocks down the road. Everybody else who has authored these kinds of books has played with history and fantasy. Nobody has ever tapped into the hood. Then, too, there aren't too many people that truly encapsulate the grit and grim of some of the most sadistic places on earth and the masochists that have no choice but to love it. Think about it, in some of the roughest neighborhoods around, people fucking with your safety and security just for the hell of it. In my opinion, that alone should offer golden nuggets of opportunities to get off.

As someone that is heavily into BDSM (don't worry, my plan is to break you in gently over the next few volumes, knock on wood), I know it'll take a half a day to explain the proper use of cat-o'-nines tails and restrains and the many other associating tools to a mere novice. Even if he or she does get the hang of it instantly, it would most likely take time and money to craft a worthwhile collection worth using *and* finding a willing participant patient enough to endure the trials and errors of steady practice that naturally comes with someone in training. In the hood, however, the motto is "make do with what you got."

In other words, there is no need for fancy-smancy devices. Sometimes a gun, some rope, a belt (or a wire cord) and some pent-up anger is all that is needed to let out some sadistic rage to do the trick.

Exactly what does all this mean for you? Well, my goal is that it means that by reading about my many chronic adventures in achieving a satisfying nutt, it might end up being a good time for you, too. Right in the heat of places that you might otherwise never get a chance to explore, right in the comfort and safety of where you are right now.

I've taken up enough of your time, so I will try and wrap it up. I won't make any promises that it'll be the best you every read. I will say that I won't bullshit you; that I've always strived for excellence and satisfaction and haven't gotten an iota of a complaint thus far. I will say that most of my sexual rendezvous are a far cry from the wham-bam-thank-you-ma'am norm and what I pen is grated out of 100% real life, my life. No frills, no fuss, no fillers (though I do have to warn you that some shit is stranger than fiction) and most of which I kept in chronological order, or a basic roundabout time frame.

So I say that to move towards these two things:

I wasn't always an angel, sometimes going out of my way to place a wicket burn on many of my partners.

I wasn't always a good by either like I am now as it comes to condom use. So don't try any of this at home without one.

In fact, don't try anything in this book, at home or elsewhere.

While it was spontaneous and turned out to be a *really* good time worth writing about, many other factors came into play, from where I was and who I was with to the taste in the atmosphere, etcetera, etcetera.

To ensure that everyone has a good time, I took the liberty of trying to take a creative flare to some of my storytelling. Don't worry. I am still going to hold my self-imposed promise not to add anything that wasn't there; I just never said that in being truly honest that I couldn't be entertaining *and* factual in the process, with a strong emphasis on being factual.

Some like it brutally honest.

Some like it commercial.

Some like it literary.

Others like a good back story.

Some don't.

Some just like it just as it is.

Either way, it should go without saying that I have changed the names of guilty to protect their identities.

With all those things being said, lay back, relax, and let me show you a good time in the hood.

Your Bossman,
Diesel King

A GOOD TIME IN THE HOOD

"Oh, c'mon, man, get off of it! Let's keep this shit street real," I said in a low and thuggish voice. I was standing right there in front of his sweet face stroking my throbbing hard denim-covered pipe down the side of my bulky thigh. "This is the only reason you even brought your happy-ass out of the house in the first place. Ain't that right?"

I lunge my pelvis at him and laughed as Rake recoiled from the edge of the bed to the middle of it.

"Might as well go ahead and admit it, partna," I continued. "We all saw how you took care of our boy Loc. You just wanted to get a taste of it."

"And as you can see we got plenty of samples for you to try," said my man Lance with a slight laugh.

Rake sat erect kneeing the middle of the bed and looked around at the roomful of men that encircled him with pure fear written across his face. He had no choice. No matter how hard he tried to turn away, he was surrounded by masculine big boy after masculine big boy with thick logs snaking around in their pants.

Shortly after my high school graduation, my running buddies and I spent the latter part of our last summer together discovering that if give the chance a lot of the dudes from our old neighborhood would have happily scraped their knees to give each of us head. Of course, for us, their recipients, this was only as a "last" resort when either of us was "desperate" enough to drain our balls that way. With a crew that usually ran eight or nine deep, ranging in age from eighteen to twenty-six pumped with raging testosterone there was always someone in desperate need. From one of my boys in the thick of a day-long booty drought to some phyne girl putting her pussy on lock for one reason or another, or for the simple guaranteed assurance that nobody would get pregnant while trying to get his nutt, whatever, it didn't matter much, only that the option was out there.

It was my boy Cole that first stumbled across this golden nugget of a secret while pumping iron at the local neighborhood rec center. Tall and handsome, Cole was a coffee-colored black man built out of what seemed like pure solid rock, a reflection of his former quarterback days. So, it came as no surprise that he was often hit on by love struck women and queers that wanted him to play a starring role in their sensual fantasies. It was no surprise either when normal guys tried to cop a look every now and again themselves. From my own personal experiences, I knew that guys overall were curious, trying to figure out if they somehow measure up to the next guy and how so? It did not necessarily mean that they guy was gay or anything like that, as much as it had to do with the struggles of the haves and have-nots. Those guys that walked around with a strut in their step like the world was their oyster with confidence and swagger, like yours truly, compared to those that did not. Topped with being naturally big and tall, in-shape guy, guys and girls were anxious in find out if everything else was anatomically correct. Couple that with being a handsome guy and a popular athlete, and those like me, being the tallest, most athletic to the most muscular we often had visitors that "accidentally" stumbled into our locker room, from the coaches on the field to the nerds on the debate team.

In the case of Whyte Myke, our token babyface white boy, that wanted so bad to be black that it hurt, he was all about sneaking a peek to find out if black was bigger, badder, and ultimately better.

Cole tried not to put much weigh behind Whyte Myke snooping around and checking him out in the changing area, being that the boy was obviously curious. There was every reason he should have been, because just like me Cole had a big floppy dick nestled between two long hanging balls when soft. The only difference between him and me, aside from a slight shift in shape, was that he was cut and I was not.

At any rate, Cole was ready to let it go as the same old same old. That is until the usual quick glances he got from other people became a full-fledge staring contest with Whyte Myke. Cole was already pumped up and a bit horny, knowing that after he put on his clothes that he was going to hook up with some girl that was guaranteed to give him some. But with

Whyte Myke standing there with his mouth wide open with drool hanging out, Cole wanted to see what the white boy was crazy enough to do it. Cole never thought Whyte Myke would call his bluff and suck his dick.

I think Cole was initially embarrassed that he was quite satisfied with Whyte Myke and his head-given skills. Given my own experience that was to come a few days later, I understood why. For a bunch of horny teenagers, we thought we were doing good just by having sex with a bunch of girls and then bragging to our friend about how good it was. I don't think it ever occurred to us that it could go beyond the scope of that. The boy didn't just play with some dick with his mouth; he was a vacuum with it, milking it for everything it was possibly worth. And when it was about time to cum, there was no need to pull out and jack off the rest, the boy not only caught it in his mouth but swallowed it like it was Hawaiian Punch and Sunny Delight. Something we thought of as a rare bird back then. And if that wasn't enough, Whyte Myke devoted minutes afterwards to cleaning dick with his mouth—something that just made us hard all over again.

It was only after Cole and another one of my friends discovered that he was sucking off each other did the two eventually quit him, only for him to start a new trend with me and the other guys in our groups, not knowing about the other. It became a double blow once we also found out that it wasn't even about us. The boy didn't care if his dick had a name or a face. He just had a thirst for black dick and white cum in his mouth. Obviously, he still remained our go to guy throughout that summer whenever we needed to dump a load, but we soon found out that they were just as eager in our own race right there in our own neighborhood.

The crew and I were in heaven finding guys after awhile that wanted nothing more than to wrap their lips around our meaty pieces. It started with some of the skinny guys that idolized us as athletes, and then moving on to average and other big guys that wanted so bad to be us. Most were content with only sucking. Others wanted a little bit more.

All indicators pointed to this dude named Scooter being the first one to get his shit packed in. Scooter was a straight-up choir boy sissy that whenever he got one of his prior suck-offs alone he would shamelessly ask to work on the dick again. Scooter wasn't as good as Whyte Myke, but he was to his credit much more enthusiastic about it. When he got on his knees, he toted up his butt and slapped it himself. We knew what was up, but we were still getting mad pussy from women to even considering indulge him. Though we did let him know that we might be interested somewhere down the line by coping a feel on that phat booty of his. The unspoken consensus was that if anybody got poked it was going to be that country bumpkin from Alabama named Ray-Ray that moved in with his sister and her family to work in the big city. Ray-Ray was cool. He was just slightly off, in the sense that he stuck out like a sore thumb from the way he dressed to the way he talked and the way he snooped around the Cut (usually an out of the way area, particularly a small would area somewhere in an urban environment) at night apparently looking to get into something. And while it was becoming clear that we were about to swarm in on Ray-Ray, the first dude in my neighborhood to give it up to me was Macho.

Every neighborhood has one. In the white neighborhood, he might be the bully that robbed a kid of his lunch money and grew up to be a bank robber. In our neighborhood, he was the kid that flipped off the teacher and had a second home in in-school suspension. He grew into his full beard and angry-at-the-world snarl that he perfected in the mirror in the county jail, terrorized the neighborhood once he got out and was ready to pulverize anybody that he felt didn't believe that he would. I was fortunate enough never to have had a run-in with him or his notorious violent temper, something that I feared and respected, although I slightly dwarfed his thick build.

I began noticing as I moved through the ranks of sports that my interaction with him, though brief, increased...especially after high school and during my brief stint playing minor league baseball. It hardly drew what I would call a crowd, even though we were a winning team. Nevertheless, Macho was always there in the strands kicking back a tall can of malt liquor and some nachos. Then, after the game, he would trail me back to the old neighborhood without even saying a word as we bus-hopped home. At first, I thought he was gaming to rob me, being that I was on the very of doing something positive with my life in a neighborhood where most men grew up to be dope heads or dope dealers. Much to my surprise that was never his intent, quite the opposite. Because I was on the verge of breaking out of there, he acted as protection to make sure that no one else messed that up. He later confessed that he had a soft spot for the game, knowing the stats of me and my teammates and knowing who was primed to go to the pros.

With all this being said, it was hard to turn down a private invitation to his crib. I had no idea what to expect. I was pleasantly surprised though by the luxurious layout of his place. We pretty much sat around and chilled, eating and drinking. Somehow or another we got off on this tangent talking about this girl on television that reminded us of the crown jewel of the neighborhood, this girl named Miranda. Neither one of us got with her, though we reminisced about our many failed attempts but started talking about our many successful conquests. Many surrounded the same girls with a few of them being around the same time.

It got me a little heated in a good way, especially when he disclosed that he and his boy had tag-teamed this phyne married woman known to be the "Mrs. Jones" of the neighborhood. The thought of his mannish ass and his pimp-like friend double-fucking her caused me to excuse myself to the bathroom. I barely got my hardened dick through the zipper to rub one out before Macho followed me in.

I didn't have a chance to say a thing. He just came right in with a cheesy grin, and said, "Damn, boy! You carrying some dick ain't you?" I was still trying my best to find some words when he decided to come on over to me and started massaging my dick with his calloused hands. He did this for a long time massaging the shaft and the balls to the point I was freely breaking precum. He followed up with something that if I wasn't there to witness I would have never believed. He went down on me. He tried to come off as a pro but had the clumsy enthusiasm of a first-timer like Scooter. He didn't make me cum. He did however do a great job once he allowed me to start coaching him.

Like I said, his head was cool. But I was getting a weird hankering for some ass. I wasn't talking about wet pussy. I was talking about some tight ass. Of course, I was honored that he sucked me off but I was still too relatively scared of him to proposition him like that. So my mind was either on taking Scooter up on his offer or ask Macho to help me take down Ray-Ray in the Cut. I was already committed to do this when I looked over at the counter and saw this big ol' jar of Vaseline. "I bet this was the shit you're boy use to slide on in her ass," I said, referring to his tryst with the married woman from across the way. "I can't tell you how many assholes this has let me ski in." I was looking for him to agree so I could proposition him on my plan. But he slipped with this look on his face, asking me if I busted open the ass of some dude before. "Shit yeah," I said in a secure macho bravado that was not my own, acting as if I did it all the time with both guys and girls. Because of his slip up and this small window of opportunity, I told him that people let me do it all the time because it looked promising that not only would I go pro but might be one of the best in the game. Who wouldn't want to be added to that scorecard?

The wheels were churning so loudly in his head that I cautiously asked if he wanted to be inducted into my "Hall of Fame." Macho went through the usual channels of telling me that he never sucked dick before, and making me promise not to tell or bodily harm would come to me and my career capping it all off with that he was in no way, shape or form a punk. He happened to tell me all this while shucking off his clothes and bending over the sink in front of me. I lubed up my dick and his puckered hole with the petroleum jelly. He bitched and moaned with every centimeter I sunk into his tight little hole. I originally thought I was putting a hurting to this thug epitome as I tried to nestle it in. I soon figured out that he was just showing out for me. Once I realized this, I simply put the screws to him, ramming the hell out of his ass and leaving in it a huge ball-draining deposit.

It took a couple of decades, before everything needed to be label, that I discovered Macho was always a proud masculine bottom with a penchant for beefy masculine manly men on the low, destroying my dreams of being his first. Up to this day, however, I am the only guy younger than him to ever get the goods.

With the baddest guy in the neighborhood riding my dick, I figured everybody else would tumble like dominoes. I would be lying if I said that every man gave in. I got my fair share of rejections regularly. Compared to what I got, however, and how I got them, I wasn't boohooing too badly. Add to that the every–growing scrolls of names that my boys were getting it weren't that uncommon for some of us to get some everyday after every nutritious meal and accompanying snack and dessert. We thought we were being noble by hemming up one guy at a time believe that we were their first for the day. We soon started comparing notes and accepted that accept that bitches like Scooter and Whyte Myke and Trey and Monkeybread, just to name a few, were just some cum-hungry motherfuckers. We thought, at the time, we were doing big things by stepping up our game by double- and triple-teaming them at the same time. It took us a full minute to realize that there demands were to supply themselves with as much dick and cum they could swim in it. They were just merely insatiable. So the crew and I decided to strengthen our brotherhood by running trains on these "insatiables". Not giving a flip if we were heating them up or cooling down their appetite for dick. We were making generous donations to the sperm bank that were their eager mouths and willing asses, with the multiple overflow being wiped into their hair and across their faces, backs, and bruised asses, or wherever there wasn't a ribbon or a dollop of cum splattered.

We eventually began to decide that with the endless supply of men we had there was no need to only run trains, or gangbang, the Insatiables. We needed to run trains on the other ninety-five percent. The pending brick wall that we ran into was that, unlike the Insatiables, most of these men had beef with admitting to working on one dick much less attempt to work on more than that. The other factor that came into play was that these were guys from our neighborhood. If they were to be trained it would be by guys in the neighborhood that would pull there Ho card whenever they could because the law of our land, if it was that easy to get it'll always be that easy to take; whether he's up to giving it up it or not. In our defense, we tried to be straight-up with these guys. We had a couple of guys to bite like Tide and QT, but for the most part everyone shied away from the proposition. Even those that we were sure were game and just needed a little convincing. To remedy the situation, we took a back-to-basics approach, letting the guy know that his secret was safe. Although a lot of stuff went down in The Cut, a strong number of guys found comfort behind four walls to do what they do best. So let's say if he lived in a crowded place and I took him back home with me, I would get him alone in my room while I had the gang in another room or coming in through the open back door undetected. Or if I was lucking to find him with a home alone, I would have friends that would slowly drop on by until there was a houseful of men. Either way, the scenario went down with the same intent of trying to turn him out. We wasn't the kind to pounce on the unsuspecting fuck, we wanted to see if we could chip away at him and hope he might cave in.

There were only a handful of guys that were ready to fight there way out of the situation, even if they were visibly turned on. They didn't know it, at the time, but it wasn't that deep at all. Some, after some time, changed there minds and wanted to lower the number of dudes. There were even a small group of guys that felt intimidated into it. Between them, they split into several smaller groups. There were those that let us fuck them but never got into it. There were those that took some time getting warmed up around the third or fourth dick before throwing it back like a bitch in heat. And then there were those that vowed only to give head.

But it was the majority that surprised me. When we came to many of them straight up with the idea, the consensus was hell no. The moment it was put under their noses, they groaned in pure fear yet fascinated and turned on by the raw masculinity surrounding them, eased into the idea of being used by burly men, taking care of a sea of penises better than many of the Insatiables. It went without question, of course, that once some of these guys got the full grasp of everything how they let loose, many of them tried to reclaim their manhood by being a top the next go around.

Even though some of us had the time of our lives talking some of these guys into submission. It wasn't even about getting a nutt after some time. It was about our fraternal bond, showing off our bravado and stamina and picking up a few tricks along the way. Because of this, we knew that there was this unwritten and unspoken rule that some men were off limits, including those that were in our private stash.

Most of the guys in our cliques kept a guy or two that they messed around with out of the fray, for one reason or another. Some of us were foolish enough to consider ourselves in love with some of them, making a strong distinction between those that we humped and those we marked as our own. The other half never laid claimed to being in love, but selfishly kept certain people out of our clutches for their control.

The one that took the cake was this dude we called Rake. Rake was a smart dude that was always coming up with some successful scheme to make money. One of which was to rake folk's yards, hence the name. Aside from being incredibly smart, Rake was also incredibly good-looking with his caramel skin with brown hair and brown eyes to match. In our book, as our crazy phrase went, he was *handsome pretty*. Handsome for a man, too damn pretty for a fuck—but you will. As things went, Rake was an overall tease that was later claimed by my prison-muscled boy Blaque for his private stash. Word soon came down the pipe that he was secretly messing around with Loc, a stout muscular guy that thought Rake was only in his private stash. When shit hit the fan, Black and Loc started going at it. Being the only one big enough to single-handedly split the two up, I suggested that his phyne ass be shared by everyone.

I devised a plan where both Blaque and Loc confronted Rake, and "sweet-talked" him into sucking them both off at the same time. While Blaque and Loc were both getting their "apologies", I was sneaking a larger-than-usual crowd of guys through the back door, busting in right when the two of them were busting their nuts in his sweet face.

"Don't be looking all sour-faced now," I said defensively to Rake, running away from the denim-covered penises that surrounded him on the bed. "Where was all that disgust when you were just serving up my boys?"

"Yeah, mofo, kind of hard to be high and mighty with cum running off the side of your face," Ray-Ray said in his southern drawl.

Rake was a smart boy. He needed no explanation of why we were there and what was expected to go down.

I knew, because of this, that he wasn't going to put up much protest. Like I said before, he was handsome pretty, and more often than not dudes boldly approached those kinds of men. The intent was not always blatantly implied. It was just there in the waves and undertows of the flirtation. And since he tempted not one but two well-known guys, he was in some deep shit. Even if he convinced us not to go through with it, there was no way he could escape a beat down. Then, too, he would have to watch his back wherever he went because sooner or later someone was going to help themselves to his ass before the whole block decided it wanted in too. The only difference, if done that way, it would be relentless. If it was done my way, he might be tagged as a ho, but as the group in our neighborhood would see it, his betrayal would be forgotten.

"Well, shit, you got a point," Rake said with an heir of cockiness. "Let me finish up with Lock and Blaque first, then let me holler at Cole, Diesel, Monster and Lance before we get this party started right."

Rake looked at us and smiled.

I flashed a smile back once I caught wind of what he was up to.

"Alright, everybody else clear out, we got some business to take care of." I said, listening to the groans and swears of about fifteen or so men exiting the room.

I knew Rake was smart, but he was teetering on the edge of being an evil genius. Not only did he want to start off with a low number, he had the sense to keep the heavy-hitters behind. Each and every one of us had big swimming dick that we knew how to use. There were many others in the mixed that were packing as well, some breaking just as even as the rest of my crew. The problem with most them was that they didn't really know how to use the equipment they were blessed with. They thought fucking was an arms race. On the flip side, there were those that had average or unique-looking dicks from skinny and long to short and beer-can fat that knew how to fuck yet wasn't blessed with the overall package. But to keep us behind meant that he wanted to get stretched out before every Tom Hairy Dick filled him to the brim.

"I'm starting to think you planned this out," Loc said with his finger and thumb stroking his goatee.

"A little bit," Rake admitted moving back towards the edge of the bed. "Originally I wanted your selfish ass. When you put it out there that you were just looking for places to bury your bone, I bounced. That was when your boy was trying to put me on. After Blaque did that then you started sniffing around and I got caught up. I was ready to leave the two of you in the dust when I found out about your whole fuck brigade. I figure if I got caught before I headed off to Duke, at least I would go out with a bang!"

"You definitely will do that, pimp!" Lance laughed again.

"Enough with the fucking history lessons, time for a second helping!" Blaque said gripping his fat dick in one hand and trying to bring Rake closer to it with the other.

"Open up," Monster, a sizeable black man in his own right with smooth and ultra cut muscles, egged on.

"Open wide for this big surprise!" Blaque said.

The room watched anxiously as Rake chewed on that piece of meat like it was the best thing he ever had in his mouth.

He sucked Blaque off again for about a good five minutes before Loc moved his head over to his crotch. Black pretty much let Rake do all the work. Loc decided that he was going to fuck his mouth hard. Loc wasn't so much rough with it as he was much more deliberate with every stroke.

The four of us that hadn't been sucked off began shucking off our clothes and getting into position, making sure that we had the lube on standby just in case. Rake pretty much went back and forth between Loc and Blaque occasionally getting our dicks wet in between. By the time I was able to get some true face time with him, Blaque had him on all four playing with his hole. Rake was moaning hard, with the sounds vibrating against my dick while trying to eye the glistening dicks being stroked into a tight half circle.

"I think this handsome fuck likes dick." I joked, distracting Rake from Blaque pushing his lubed dick into his ass.

With one good thrust, Blaque drove that dick down to the hilt. I was afraid that I might have to fight Rake if he accidentally tried to bite off my dick. But Rake took it like a champ, becoming more vigorous in sucking me off.

"I think the dude loves some dick." Monster said, trying to signal me to move out of the way.

Eventually, I did.

As I pulled out, Rake eagerly swallowed it into his mouth. And that was not easy feat for the most trained of dick-wetters. At half staff Monster was easily eleven inches soft. Rake must have known what it took to get him to stand at attention so fast. Monster began showing his appreciation by manhandling the back of Rake's dark brown head, easing his handsome pretty-ass face into his wide brawny lap. It was quite interesting looking at Rake like that, with a thick dick poking out of his straightened throat, trying not to gag and failing miserably at it.

"Suck that shit, punk!" Monster hissed.

Monster let go of his head. Instead of retreating, Rake tried it again, able to get even more of Monster in his mouth. It was so hot watching Rake suck him off so frantically, like his life depended on it, that neither Cole nor Lance even both to wedge their way in on the action.

"Yeah, suck that dick, punk," Monster panted and sucking his teeth before, "oh, damn!"

It took us a second for us to figure out that Monster had let a nutt go off in his mouth. The way Rake steadily cleaned him off, the way he was still sucking him off, we would have never known anything if it hadn't been for sputtering heaves Monster was expelling.

Lance caught on first, pushing Monster out of the way and forced Rake onto his crotch. Rake wasn't nearly as eager to take care of Lance as he was Monster and I. Lance didn't really give a shit one way or another ordering Rake to lick his balls and back again, with Cole slapping the sides of his flesh-sucking face with his dick.

"Damn, man, you really do know how to work the meat off of a dinosaur bone." Cole rumbled moments later against the backdrop of Rake loudly slurping his own skin.

"If you think that's good, get a load off of his ultra grip ass!" Blaque offered.

He was still back there hammering into him like a fool against Rake. Every inch of him was dripping with pouring sweat, grunting and groaning about how that piece of handsome pretty ass was his fine fuck, probably never working so hard a day in his life.

"This here is about to make me loose it, man," Blaque said sinking his dick into him. "I'm going to bust that pussy wide open with this nutt!"

Blaque dug his fingers into Rake, and with a few hard strokes let loose in his ass. Obviously, it was too much for Cole as he busted off in his mouth with Lance pulling out and busting a nutt right in his face.

I laughed aloud, missing my turn to get back in on the action as Loc replaced Blaque and Monster replaced Cole. I moved back to where Loc was filling Rake up to the hilt with every hard stroke, letting him know he was just as committed to screwing him as he was trying to screw with the friendship Blaque and Loc.

Loc definitely put the screws to him going from power-fucking Rake to doing some super-duper power-fucking that made me question whether he was part machine, too. Keep in mind, Loc did this all the while Cole got sucked off, Blaque got cleaned up, and Monster knowing that I was behind Loc went again.

For awhile I thought I would never get a crack at Rake's ass, splattering my dick with several makeshift lubes scatted across the room because I knew the way Loc was going at it, he was on the verge of fucking Rake dry. Loc eventually came. But he screeched it out as loudly that I was already humping Rake a good while by the time sound popped back into my ears. Usually I was a beast with it, up there with Blaque and Loc, thinking of a piece of ass as nothing more than a vessel to service my dick. So it threw those that thought they knew me well off when I flipped Rake on his back, lifted his legs and started putting a slow burn on him with my lingering fuck. I hadn't gone soft by any means. I had foresight on my side, knowing there were soon going to be a room littered with men trying to outdo the other by putting the screws to him, or at least perpetrated hard as if they did. Why not give Rake something to remember other than a sore ass? I probably stayed inside of Rake just as long as Loc, if not longer before ultimately losing my battle to my own nutt. Where I went long and strong, Cole made up for gentleness by humorously bucking Rake like he was taking on a wild bronco, making him shoot almost instantly.

Monster went after that, then Lance.

I decided to give Rake a two-minute break, knowing that on the other side of that door was vultures eager to leave their mark.

We opened up the room to the rest of the guys. When one guy finished with his ass, there was always another guy shoving him out of the way and taking his turn. The line moved so steadily it became one big blur of men climbing off of his back and later using his mouth to clean themselves up. And with cum steadily gushing out of his ass, Rake was quite busy lapping up cum from the countless dicks that stretched out his hole. This continued next to four hours with Rake showing his like or dislike with the guy by either throwing it back stroke for stroke or either lying there taking it like a beached fish. After what was supposed to have been the last man I couldn't resist adding my load one more time, probably the fifth or sixth that night. Above anything else, I was turned on by the relatively medium-skinned black man's ass turning beet red. I started slow dicking him again, listening to him tell me that even with all the dick he took and the slimy mess I was swimming in, that it still felt good to him, like home. It was enough to send me over the edge to cap off our day and let my sore dick rest for an eternity.

Unbeknownst to us at the time, Rake would be our grand finale of the summer season before everyone began parting ways. We fought hard to keep our new favorite pastime going, but with most of the neighborhood being tapped and everybody wanting to become a willing participant before going off to college or trade school, it took the fun out of coaxing some to give it up to a room full of men.

While libidos still ran high for those wanting on their ticket to get out, it wasn't uncommon for us to get a threesome or a foursome going. The biggest party that we were able to get going was a seven-man orgy starring two bottoms, with one being this youth pastor that would go on to start one of those mega churches and the other being this budding music producer that would go on to have a very successful career.

HOURS AFTER THE BAR CLOSES

2:44AM

Fifteen minutes before last call ends, I am standing on the sidelines as a wingman to a black leather master getting sucked off this light skinned boy putting in his application to be his new slave. The boy is on his knees, nervous as fuck, patiently bobbing his head back and forth on the beer-can wide prick. The boy is no virgin by any means, giving blowjobs out on the dance floor like it was free candy to popping his jaw to accommodate awkward-shaped dicks like his. This is the first time I have seen him up close and the only time I have seen him with a mouthful. Yet there is this sort of jene ne sais quoi feeling that rolls off of his aura that suggest he is at home here. Sated like a motherfucker. The boy doesn't need to be told twice to watch his crooked teeth on the foreskin or to work his tongue deeper into the fat piss slit. The boy isn't nervous that the master won't call him back for an interview. He knows based on skills alone he will start first thing Monday morning.

The boy is nervous because he knows better than anybody that it is against the rules to eye me, stroking my exposed dick while, at the same time, tending to his new boss.

2:49AM

The black leather master starts to labor deep heavy breathing. Nothing like I had ever heard, a cross between a sigh and a moan and a grunt. His eyes are welded shut alluding to the fact he is sure to cum soon.

2:51AM

Nothing ever cums and the boy upstage him with his loud slurping and these throat-gurgling ticks.

2:53AM

My new master friend sighs and groans, grunts and moans and curses as he holds the back of the boy's head. The way he screeches he sounds like he let go of a half-gallon, and laughs at the boy who can't gulp it all down.

2:55AM

The boy finish cleaning him up, even licking up the extra running out of the creases of his mouth.

2:56AM

The boy rises to his feet in shame, not able to look at me or the leather man in the eye.

The leather man shoos him away with a twenty-dollar bill and sends him to buy our last round for the night.

The boy is out of earshot when the leather man asks me what I think. Before I am able to speak my peace, he informs me that he will be throwing him back to the "stroll" from which he came from. When I ask why, the leather man states that he doesn't tolerate disrespect of any kind, particularly from no whore.

"If he's going to eye your dick while sucking on mine, he doesn't need disciple. He needs a fucking orgy!"

2:59AM

The boy returns with our drinks.

3:01AM

The boy is steadily eyeing me, but tries to save face with the leather man by agreeing to drink his piss in the back.

3:13AM

On the hunt for some action of my own.

3:21AM

Think my search has ended with this doe-eyed Asian boy that naively curious to the scene.

3:26AM

I am spitting game and got him laughing. I don't want to come off like I'm just looking for a lay (though it wouldn't hurt).

3:29AM

The boy tires to intervene. It is obvious that the leather man gave him his walking papers shortly after taking a leak across his face.

3:39AM

Agree to get the cute Asian boy to join me for coffee and doughnuts from around the way. His bitchy friend, whom he rode with isn't too keen on leaving him with a stranger. Totally understandable. I invite him to tag along, too. My treat. He is adamant in his response, making up some lame story about heading off to work in a few hours. The Asian boy wants to tell his friend he'll be okay with me, but instead vouches to give me his number. His friend is still mean-mugging me like I done him wrong. I check the memory bank to see if I have. He doesn't register in my mind, leaving me to believe that he is either looking out for his friend or looking to be his lover one day in the near future.

3:45AM

Try to track down piss boy, thinking if he likes it in the face he might love it up the ass.

3:53AM

The bar is about to close, not having any luck finding some luckless runt to follow home.

4:06AM

Out in the parking lot catching up with some old friends that I hadn't seen in awhile. I still keep my eyes out for some straggling prospects, only to spot the weird loner and the ugly mofo that you gave dick to when you were piss drunk and somehow thinks that you're his boyfriend.

4:16AM

A little tired heading towards the expressway home. My horniness overrides it, thought. I know that somewhere out there in the city is two fleshly mounds that have my name in the groove of its valley. Where?

4:34AM

My dick is already hard. Been so since I made up my mind that this is the place I am going to get my "release." It his harder than ever, eager in anticipation.

Aside from the bulge in my pants, I have to play it cool. I think about baseball to cool it down.

Bad idea, bats and balls.

Basketball.

Another bad idea, a sport that condones men for dribbling balls.

Football.

Let's not even go there.

My dick dies at the thought of ballet and orchestra, and anything else that is not macho, manly. Perfect.

It gets me enough cool to make my entrance into the coffee lounge. Giving men that had come before me a reason to smile and men about to leave time to reconsider.

4:52AM

I move from the lounge down to the locker room where I am shameless followed by a handful of men with stiff sticks and humid holes. I indulge them all by walking slowly. Though my firm full ass is never used, it is a grand muscular tease. Perhaps, second only to my swinging piece, it is the kind of serious thrust I put behind each and every one of my fucks.

4:56AM

I barely get my shirt off before I am approached by the muscularity of a hairy daddy that introduces himself as _____. He is a well built, sexy-ass mofo with a very thick accent. He can be Russian or Ukrainian or whatever other country over there that ends in "stan." Not even for a white man, but for a man in general, he is equipped with some amazingly mean dick, strutting around naked like he is cock of the walk.

He is jonesin' for some young black booty, but I politely decline without starting an international or racial incident that my preference is for myself. Letting him know that I would happily swim in his sloppy seconds and would be honored if he swam in mine.

5:01AM

I finally get all of my clothes off and stuff them in a locker. My first reaction is to find my room and leave my locker room key in there. That is too obvious, I reason, choosing to head to the showers and wash away the bar with this complimentary soap and sponge.

5:09AM

I notice that I got a couple of admirers watching me in the showers like I am an endangered species.

I am eager to ignore them.

They are not my type and are too Mandingo happy, giving out stage whispers that they wish there Little Red Riding Hood and I was the BIG BAD WOLF with the HUGE BLACK COCK that would ravish them in the woods.

5:12AM

I decide to play into their fantasy.

I figure if they're just going to stand there and watch might as well give them a show. I cover myself from head to toe with suds and began stroking my soapy dick.

5:14AM

Motherfucking minutemen! I think, wanting to laugh but settle a "gotcha" smile.

The two of them came like fire hoses on the tile floor below them. Spent all that damn money to get in and at the end had to do it for themselves.

5:17AM

I climb out of the showers still laughing at those lame motherfuckers as they have long disappeared back to the front, probably to ashamed to come back.

5:19AM

I move to my room through the semi-darkness draped in my white towel peeking through the various doors along the way. The first two doors were empty. Another was filled with sex in the oral form and another of the anal kind. And in between them is a skinny-mixed guy in a room with a huge neon green jelly dong surfing up the crack of his ass. He is lying on his stomach with his head in his arms looking the other way like he didn't give a shit who came in.

I pass on the offer and head to my room. Too many guys are standing around. One of them has got to make a move.

I get quite comfortable in my room equipped with the works: a television laced with several channels of porn, a luxurious supply of condoms and lube and disposable enemas.

5:23AM

Regret not wearing my double-thick black rubber cockring.

5:26AM

Realize that I have been here an hour and no action.

5:29AM

Scan the other rooms on the other side of mine naked and hard. Tempted by the many willing choices in between, including two very attractive black dudes. One being this gorgeous brick-colored dude with a remarkably trimmed goatee and a high bubble butt pretending to drift off to sleep. Yeah, right. The other is the manila-colored dude lubed up and stroking off to the deafening loud porn pulsating out of his room.

I am going berserks! I can't decide! Men of color aren't all that uncommon here yet it isn't all that common either. Two fairly decent-looking black men with some masculine presence are like finding a diamond in the rough and gold in the raw. In spite of this conundrum, something in my head told me to check on the guy with the crowded doorway.

5:32AM

Sure enough, nobody had the balls to venture in.

A bunch of pussies! Knowing my history, I know men who fuck men had to use codes and a dark alleyway just to break off a nutt. Give them a dark and seed bar with a leg to get away with something they will jump on it like brown on natural rice. Give him a bit of light and they want to act all scared.

I don't even have to barrel on through. They part for me like they had been waiting all night, like a king making an entrance, fueling my already larger-than-life ego.

The man in the bed with the foot-long dildo meticulously placed riding between his mounds turns around to look at me as I close the door. He seems not to be impressed, turning his head back to the wall.

I have been around the block too many times to know that this is his front.

"Pull the shade down," he mutters in a silky soft but masculine tone.

"What, no show?"

"No." He pauses. "What time is it?"

"Five-thirty." I say, pulling down the window shade.

"They've been gawking since two-thirty."

He turns his head back to the door. He thinks that I am in eyesight when in fact I am at the foot of the bed looking at this green monster lying lazily across the entire length of his crack.

"Can you blame 'em?"

"Don't tell me, they're afraid of a jelly dildo?"

"Who's afraid of Virginia Woolf? Most are afraid of fucking with the real think and most don't even come close in size," I say. "Except for me, of course."

"And you're special?"

"Of course," I say rummaging through the drawer for some lube."

He tries again to look at my package as I find an extra clear bottle of lube next to the dildo.

"Nice," he says with my dick in his face.

"Suck."

5:45AM

He lifts himself up, and past his lips like a fish and gulp me in like water. He seems at a loss. His mouth is dry. He tries to get the top of it wet with his tongue, and then brings his lips into the fold to caress it.

If I still had my pants on, I could offer him a Jolly Rancher.

He, however, doesn't need it, making good use of the friction. I can't move in and out. I can move back and forth, bringing about this weird scrubbing bubbles sensation.

It doesn't feel like I'm close to cumming. It just feels like my vibrating legs got an inch. I just can't scratch.

5:58AM

Remembers he got a dildo and an ass that needs to be played with. Reach over to feel his ass.

He has one of those asses that look dense from afar but is doughy as hell in reality. Made for kneading bread, meaning that it's definitely "pushin' for the cushion."

6:01AM

He likes. His dick sucking becomes much more invigorated, and I haven't even bothered to play within the crease.

For a big black guy, I have big black hands which mean I have big black fingers. My last fuck didn't call 'em then that though. He said finger were too human for me. He called them digits. Big black motherfucking digits! Attached to a motherfucking mitt.

I stroke around Ground Zero, tingling the fine hairs and the crease leading down to the bottomless abyss just to find out that the fucker is well-lubed.

I go in, slipping in a digit and barely get back a knuckle. I slip in two digits. He smugly looks back, as if to ask 'was that the best I could do?'

A couple of strokes against his fat little hotspot, he is trying to muffle his gasps and groans with my dick.

6:08AM

He plays it cool, not at all suspecting that I am just a finger away from freeing his inner bitch.

"AhhhhHHHH!" He screeches, letting my dick fall out of his gorgeous mouth.

"So there's the charm?" I offer calmly.

He hits high notes and low notes and notes only the prissy of dogs can hear. I don't even care any more. His ass lips are like quicksand to my digits and they forgot how to stay calm.

"That's feels like a big dick right there, doesn't it?"

He squirms beneath my digit whimpering and partying like an injured dog.

"Oh, c'mon, my fingers up your ass ain't nothing compared to the freak-down you're about to give this dildo!"

I pull my finger out, watching his gaping hole slowly close shut.

"Uh-un," I say to it as it is about to close up.

I quickly pick up the foot-long jelly dong by its half heavy balls. The only part of it that isn't lubed, and fill his slightly-resistant hole to the brim in one very violent, very brilliant stroke.

6:22AM

I hold it in place, crushing its balls against his for one solid minute, listening to him expel all his demons.

6:23AM

I pull it straight on out.

He is no longer wincing or mistaking it for a wrestling match trying to tap out. His raises his legs relax beneath him as his hole collapses like a loud fart.

He wants to spit in my face and curse me and my mama out. He is unable to for several reasons. Pain and my size inflicting more pain being two of them. The one that holds dear, the only one that matters, is truth.

Before he stepped foot in the building, he was just a fuckee wanting to test out his brand new toy. He wants to be bitched and whored like some of his size queen buddies had over exaggerated. Real was too real for him, so he figures what a better way to get notches on his belt that to get dildo-fucked in a bathhouse. How often does that happen? Besides, rubber gives to road, surely flesh in more accommodating.

Boy, oh boy, how he got his wish!

The stories he is going to tell are going to make them 'ohh' and 'ahh' each time he tells them.

Above anything else, I am most certain of this. Even the hungriest of pig bottoms in not going to supply a complete stranger a license to shove a large foreign object up their ass. Sure, for every masochist there is an equal sadist. But even the hugest dicks eventually come, a manufactured one never does.

"Geez, take it easy man!" He says trying to muster up some anger in his voice amidst the pain.

Likes it? No, no. He is fighting hard to keep it all in his skin. He loves it!

"Cum-sucking dong sluts like you don't have much say so in the matter."

6:29AM

He takes a very deep breath and lets it all out, with the head of the dildo rubbing over his greased puckered hole. It becomes apparent after a few tries that this nameless fuck isn't keen for foreplay, sucking in the tip of the big-headed dildo with nothing more than his sphincter.

"Take it easy? Fuck! Seems to me I was taking it way too easy!"

He thinks he can beat me to the punch, thinks that I am going to run ram it into his chute again as he begins pumping feverously back against his powerful dildo.

"Hungry-ass motherfucker, ain't you?" I say, watching his ass try to devour the dildo in these freaky gyrations.

He doesn't understand that just like the dick flanked by my legs, I am very much in control of the one of the other side of my mitts. Instead of inch by inch, he should be eternally grateful for every centimeter he receives, taking whatever I give him.

He still continues to be hardheaded, thinking he will get the dildo in his own time. So I prove my point by viciously popping out the length of the dildo to counter his winding bucks, leaving his hole to gape open and talk back demanding to be filled again.

"Looks like your hole needs this dick, don't it?"

He instructively shoved back hoping that his real ass will catch onto the fake dick.

"Yeah," he moans once he accepts that I am playing keep away with it, bouncing it from one greasy cheek to the other.

"Yeah, what."

"Yeah, sir," he says.

"I would've accepted Dick Master or Dick God, but sir's cool."

"Yes," he says as I rub it at the top of his crack, lowering his body back down to the bed.

He is letting me know that he is ready to be put down.

"No, sir," I say to both. "Keep that skinny ass up.

He obliges, waiting on his prick to fill him again with lube oozing out of his hole down to his balls.

I start etching down from the top of his crack to the budding crater that was once high tight hole, plunging him again with the dildo. He groans and squirms and wails and moans and creates other noises that are not human, as his hole is being stretched open. His dick hangs heavy and hard between his legs, thrusting him between heaven and hell and tries to find some middle ground in between. He is suffering from this amuck because the last stubborn ring in the nether region of his hole will not succumb.

I push forward anyway though, through his screaming pain to his mumbling pleasure and back again. I snake it in further and deeper and harder and faster, twisting it and jamming it in until his sounds mirrors my ever-changing mood.

At the rough speed I am going my arms should be exhausted, my mitts cramped, but they aren't. I am too enthralled with the dildo vanishing into the abyss to care about anything else.

"Don't run from it, fool." I say smiling as he scoots up the bed attempting the separate his battered ass from the pounding dildo. "I got you so wide open I'm thinking about directing traffic through your ass."

He is so open that it is ridiculous. Practically next to nothing is stopping the balls of the jelly dong from disappearing up his ass, too. He lets out all his excitement and angst through his mouth while his body starts trembling wildly.

"Got that shit up in you now!"

"Oh, God," he yammers.

"Oh, Goddamn is right. I ain't finished with you yet. Keep your hands on the board. Not only am I going to cum without jacking off, I'm going to make you shoot just from the memory of it."

He might be confused, but understands enough to keep quiet. He grabs a hold of the headboard tighter cursing the saints and expelling the demons.

"You're a real-live slut, ain't you?" I ask.

"Yeah," he sobs.

"You're a pussy-ass slut."

"Yeah,"

"Then taking all this dick is nothing to a slut like you ain't it?"

"Yeah," he breaths.

"No," I correct. "A bitch-ass pussy slut like you is already taking a limousine worth of dick already."

"It isn't real," he huffs.

"It isn't? Didn't it open you up like one? Make you spread your legs open like a 7/11? 24/7? 365 days a year and 52 weeks? I can go on?"

"Uh-huh."

"Uh-huh, what?"

"Dick Master…uh-huh, Dick Master."

"See, you just admitted it. It's real dick forcing its way up your sweet sugar-coated ass, invading you like you never have been invaded before! It is the only dick in the world that s made to satisfy a bitch in heat like you!"

"Oh," he groans as I once again slam it hard back into him.

"It's the only one in the world that is hungry for a sloppy slutty hole like yours as you are for big dicks."

He winces a bit, taking my words in at the same rate he is taking it, fast and hard.

"And the beautiful thing about it is that it's my dick. My big dick is the one that is making mush out of your sweet hole. Ruining you for every other man that comes after me."

"Oh, God," he howls.

"Damn, right," I say. "I can open the door and let every…fuck… takes a crack at this ass and you'll still be numb next to this one, my one."

"Oh, fuck me."

"You've been fucked you slut."

"Oh," he goes again.

"You pussy-ass bitch. Give it up!"

"Oh, God," he stammers over and over and over again.

He is close to the edge. Time to make my move.

To get him to cum with no assist, without touching himself is nothing more than a good massage to the prostate. To make him cum with absolutely nothing poking him but the memory of it sounds like some cold pimp shit.

Something I just heard about it up to this point, but something that I know that is possible.

I begin leveling off the strokes I leveled off in his ass, taking my time to be meticulous in probing the exact spot of his prostate. Not the roundabout area, but the center of his orgasmic universe.

His norm changes, becoming something else altogether, something that is hard to describe yet easy to get.

I can tell he is enjoying it and doesn't want it to end, using one hard to spread open his cheek as he tries desperately to balance himself with the other hand.

I let him ride this nirvana for a moment longer, savoring every tickling stroke. My primal urge soon takes over, battering his already bothered butthole with relentless force zeroing in to this one particular spot. Even then his loud sputtering sobs are different, and much more at peace.

I am so caught up in the breathing up front that I almost fail to pay attention to what is in front of me, watching his balls drastically clamming up at the same moment his hard dick swells even bigger. And with a few more concise pumps I pull the monster dong straight out of his hole.

At first, my blood rises in disappointment, knowing that I brought him close enough to the edge for him to let go of a nutt. I am not looking for Niagara Falls, just a measly squirt of that. My hopes soon renews with him throwing it back, still on the receiving end of his beautiful dick.

But in a strange twist of fate, he starts gripping louder than ever before, bucking the raw humid air wildly as he strains his legs over again to brace himself for more.

The next thing I know he strains his voice in a silently audible scream that ends with a long ropey mess spewing from between his legs. The initial jet barrels out in a violent rush to the bed beneath him while the rest drips out thick and slow like maple from a tree.

The amazing part about it all isn't that I got him to nutt pure from the memory of getting fucked. It is that the sticky slim didn't not spurt from over here to over there. It is that it stays one long continuous ribbon that in the end stretches about two feet respectively.

"That was fucking hot." I say.

"Yeah," he breaths, "your turn."

7:39AM

He offers to help me cum.

I decline.

I feel that just busting a nutt to the backdrop of our steamy rendezvous will ruin what we worked so hard to accomplish.

His nutt was special. In comparison, I knew mine will not.

I can tell in his voice he wants to thank me properly, he wants me to stay, but I have something else on my mind.

7:42AM

I open up the window blind and leave his room to an even larger crowd standing outside of his door with there dicks out. Unlike before, where I was welcomed like royalty, I am ignored, having to fight my way out as every man around looks at him with his ass up and dildo fully impaled in his ass.

His thanks to me.

7:44AM

I am back in my room, still relishing in my accomplishment as I pick up a white town and head off to the sauna for the Sunrise Breakfast.

The cashier raved about it earlier.

It is the hours between six and eight when the bathhouse opens its door to the patrons for free.

The cashier went on to tell me that it was second only to the late evening rush, champion in by chained-by-the-balls men and hounds too lazy to cruise, that business professionals come in for their news and "morning brew." He gave me fair warning that by me being, black, articulate, and built like a Titan that could be the toast of the town or very well taken care of in the wallet by some corporate bastard that needs to be taken down a peg or two.

Since, originally, I wasn't planning on staying this long, might as well find out.

8:02AM

On my fifty try of going back there; I stick my head in the sauna to find a full house. It is so crowded back there it isn't funny. Under any other circumstances, I should stick out like a lighthouse in a corn field. This go around, I am just a sprinkle on top of a berry-flavored smoothie filled with tattooed villains and twinks, pierced bad boy and muscled daddies. Stroking off in one corner, blowing off in another. Even my hairy Russian friend from earlier is tagging the ass of the black boy that was jagging off to the loud porn while many drape towels over their faces and used the rooms for its original purpose. Race isn't even a factor, looking out at the Rainbow Coalition that it covered, white and black and brown and yellow and red with a couple of albinos of the races.

8:05AM

My feet lead me to the door of the massage room. I am tempted to go in, but I heard once that part of the "total relaxation" technique is to get me off by hand. I cannot cum that way, not after all that I have seen in the last few hours. So I take a detour to the baths. Then take another up the stairs to the clothing optional deck.

8:08AM

I have no intention of stripping off my clothes once I get up there. There is no need. Most likely given that it is already daylight, and considering where the building is to the surrounding skyscrapers even the brazen of exhibitions aren't that bold.

8:09AM

Hate to say it. Boy, am I wrong!
The rooftop is covered with mostly decent-bodied naked men. A good part of the extended multicultural population is sitting around taking a sunbath and looking on as the other half is somewhere in the middle putting a new spin on an old game, going from sitting on one hard dick to another in a free-for-all smorgasbord.

8:12AM

I am propositioned by this skinny older black man standing nearby. He is about sixty plus years old. He is older-looking without exactly looking his age. Though it isn't a big secret, even with a full head of silver-blue hair. In a former life he could have been a dancer of sorts, still firm and sporting a Prince Albert proudly in his lounge chair. Everything but his face is handsome, so his strong conversation isn't enticing. And being that he breaths money and talks money, puts me off at the same rate as his condescending tone to my youth and muscular build.

8:19AM

I try easing away from him without telling him off. I refuse to come off like the ass he is. He has a full patent on that. However, he becomes much more intriguing by the second with the arrival of his new naked friend.

He too is about sixty plus and black and in fairly good shape. But the comparisons end there. Whereas his asshole of a friend is on the thin and trim side, he has a round face and plump solid muscular body that is almost frightening. He doesn't have beach muscles like most of the gym bunnies up here. His is toned from years of plowing the fields and picking cotton in the ways of the Old Deep South. Ways he tries to shed by shaving his head and growing this thick gruff handlebar moustache and goatee that hangs and an inch or four off of his chin. Looking like he is more at home on a motorcycle gang than any place else. Even his full tattooed belly is muscled and narrows down to a comely V-shape. I try not to look any further down than that, but it is hard not to. His thighs are enormous. They were made for bucking. What is flopping down between then isn't bad either. Even through the eyes of a confirmed top it is incredible. I mean, he has the stuff the most insatiable size queen would never dream of. Something that is as thick as a painter's wrist and almost as long as his forearm too. Talk about hung!

8:23AM

He tries to engage me in conversation. His friend, his suspected lover, continues to interject.

When his friend turns away, he motion me over to the edge of the building to where he is heading.

8:27AM

I have no problems admitting that though he is significantly older than me, but at least a couple of scores, I am very much attracted to him. Lustful, yes. It is so much more than that, though. Wordlessly, he makes me feel comfortable because he is comfortable with himself. He has no reason to advertise his hard masculinity, it just is. It is him and he is it. He is an all-natural, slightly hairy man that enjoys the company of other men, naked. He does a great job of being him, being natural such, a rare treat in this world, that I forget apart of my fear of heights standing next to him near the retainer wall, as he smiles at me with a cup of orange juice in his mitts.

"So," he starts off. His voice is a deep baritone laced with enough bass that it is solid and firm without straining of harshness. "New?"

"No," I lie.

"I meant to the decade," he jokes.

He engages me deep in conversation, as if we were both in a business conference instead of in our birthday suits.

My dick as hard as a rock to the sound of his voice and the words that comes out of it.

The sex card is not playable, I reason mournfully in my head.

There is no way he is bottoming for me. He has a dick that he wants to use, and even if I am willing to give it up for to him, for the first time, out of pure respect, he is just too big to even consider it in the back or in the front.

I am so revved up about him because he is me, everything I am and want to be.

I want to kiss him.

I want to hold and kiss him.

It might mislead him into thinking that I want more than that, and I don't want to be a fuck-tease.

Our eyes lock.

It isn't the first time. It is just different, more intense like predator to prey.

"You look...tense." He says.

"I am." I confess. "Standing so close to the edge isn't making me feel any more comfortable."

Good save!

"Afraid of heights?"

"Yeah," I say flustering with embarrassment letting this other big, tall, dark man know I have a fear.

"Do you feel comfortable with me?"

"Yeah," I say honestly.

"Let me try something with you to help you get over your fear."

I gulp, not deciphering whether or not he is sincere or if he is game at trying something else to get me over my fear.

He deliberately walks behind me, brings his arms around my stomach tightly with his pulsing dick pressing against my back.

I try to breathe regularly, but I am turned on by him and slightly afraid I am going to shit on him as he walks me closer to the edge.

"You feel I got you?"

"Yeah," I say.

"Open your eyes."

My eyes were open. I just wasn't looking up or down but across the interior edge of the roof.

"Look ahead," he adds. "Straight ahead."

I didn't want to come off as a punk, so I did.

"You're looking ahead?" He asks.

"Yeah," I breathe.

"Look down."

I do, and quickly the ground gets further away causing me to get dizzy.

I start to push back, but he is stronger, standing his ground. I want to tell him to move but it occurs to me that I don't know his name.

Stupid fuck!

I am so enraptured by this guy, comfortable with him and feel he is trustworthy, and I don't know his fucking name!

"Steady now, Arnell's got you."

Good. Arnell.

"Just keep on looking down, feel my arms around you. I'm a strong man with strong arms. Worked about two of your lifetimes before you even stepped out on the world. You ain't going nowhere."

9:12AM

He holds me close. My fear is not far from game. It is just subsiding, tossing me between my fear and his arms.

He must be getting tired holding me like this. I am no small man. I am not some delicate flower. I am man made from steel. The brilliant thing he is too.

I don't want to insult him by asking him to let me go, because I want neither but the morning is passing and he looks like a busy man.

9:19AM

"How do you feel up there?"
"Good. You?"
"Good."

9:22AM

His arms are tight around me. They always have been yet they seem to do more. Subtly, but more. They do not roam my hard muscle flesh as much as they seem to stroke one area or another, letting me know that he was still there.

I am unsure of what to make of it all. I don't want to jump to conclusion. I am even more confused when his dick stirs against one of my mounds slowly etching it way to my crack. Is this intentional? It is apart of his routine phase of morning wood?

My questions resolves once the scruff of his chin brushes up against my shoulder and his warm face breathes onto my neck.

"So this was the master plan?"

"Shit yeah. I can't have you afraid of heights when I'm about to teach you how to fly."

"Oh, shit."

9:26AM

I lean my head away from his mouth, giving him more access to my neck as he begins kissing it slow and seductive like.

His arms are crossed just beneath my pecs. His callous fingers begin to thumb my pointy nipples. He knows how to work them. And as much as I try, I cannot stop the gasps from coming out of my mouth.

I am in hot heat, panting and waiting on his next move as the sun kissed my face. I am anxious, he is patient. The paradox of our age group, something that escapes me for a moment but never alludes me. My greatest embarrassment is to come off as a young buck that needs to be tamed by a hard strong woof. I know from experience that those feats are golden, feeding to the ego more so than the sexual appetite.

I remember to breathe. Barely catching my breath in time to feel his hand slip down to my hardened sex and the other to the side of my waist.

"I bet you bust open a lot of assholes with this thing, huh young buck?" He says taking his hand and stroking my dick.

"Yes, sir." I say out of respect.

"When I was your age I busted a few wide open, too. My favorite of all was this cat name Jon. He was unassuming just like you. Hard and masculine front of everybody. Once I got him alone thought, he let me get up in it whenever I had the dick and grease to do so. Most times I didn't even need that. His shit just melted like butter every time I slid home."

He licks my earlobes following a series of kisses along my neck. The wet of his mouth with the warmth of his breath over it causes another moan to escape from my lips.

"I bet that ass is sweet just like his." He murmurs.

I do not respond. I just breathe deeply.

His dick is getting hard dripping wildly with precut with a trail right down the center of my crack. His dick follows from top to bottom. He feels so damn good, so damn right every time he passes my spot that taking my last stand here is crossing my mind.

"Damn, that hose is springing a leak, old man." I laugh playfully.

"Old man?" He pauses. "A tight tender like you needs all motion lotion to manage all this."

I think to say something smart but I choose not to. His is a raging bull and I am no bullfighter. I am a bull. A calf to him. A young bull, at that, eager for a challenge to prove myself, knowing that an old bull like him like to prove he still got it.

I am making up my mind to let him do it or not, and the more he rubs it pass my hole the more I want to let him do it.

I quickly change my mind now that he rubs the enormous head against my backdoor. I want to scream that I am a virgin back there. It isn't like I am lying. It is the complete and utter truth. But to tell him that is like handling him an invitation to pop my cherry, etching him into my memory for all my eternity to remember.

"Got that shit on lock like Fort Knox. Good boy." He whispers soulfully in my ear.

I feel that the danger is over.

"Don't be ashamed of getting it wet for Big Daddy. Just make him work hard to get it open. That way when he gets that shit he can claim that shit."

He begins stroking my dick soft and slow.

Using his plump pinky to knock my balls together, he asks, "Tell me, my dear boy, when was the last time you fucked somebody?"

"About a couple of hours ago."

"It feels so full."

"I wasn't the one having sex."

I explain to him the events that transpired with the man in the room with the dildo, lacing every intimate detail. He listened intently; firmly stroke me, asking me certain questions as he comes off of my shoulder. He tries to be subtle, repositioning his spit slick pipe underneath my butt crack and between my bulky tights, using his pinky to lift up my loose nutt sac so it can run under mine.

I am amaze at how good he feels. Right there. Even better than once I squeeze my thighs around him. He starts bobbing it in and out as if he is really fucking me with tenderness and care.

My mind briefly forgets my fear of heights and everyone else standing around on the rooftop. I want to tell them all that I am not being fucked. It just looks that way.

My youth, my prideful youth, my stabling establishment needs to solidify my budding dominance in this world, not my submission to succumb. Moreover the fear that others might think I can take a man so huge on a whim.

9:57AM

I no longer give a flying shit about what these motherfuckers think. We are no longer on speaking terms much less speaking the same language.

I am slick with his spit and cum.

More of the latter than the former.

The friction of this combination along with skin must be good to him. Because all I hear from the back is him huffing and puffing.

10:02AM

My breathing soon mimics his.

I somehow manage to bend over to view the streets below with my hands against the edge.

He causes me to gasp each passing stroke against my prostate passing underneath my raised sac and the crevices on the side.

10:14AM

He is so lost in himself using my body this way that he forgets about me, the man behind the thighs.

If we were truly fucking, I would be nothing more than a hole to his big black pipe.

10:20AM

He remembers me again.

10:21AM

He consciously pokes roughly at my prostate until it is sore with heat and raw with pleasure, leaving me sticky with his mess.

10:23AM

He raises me upright, cuffing my neck. His kisses are dry and brief along the way, trailing along the jaw back to the nape. He begins to seductively stroke my dick and with his mouth in my ear he asks, "When was the last time you use this thing?"

10:24AM

"The night before last." I respond releasing a gasp at my own leaky mess coming from his firm, forgiving strokes.

"Tell Big Daddy about it." He commands.

I gathered my mind, trying to remember how did it go from just words to just sex?

"Nothing special," I suggest. "It was just a fuck and a nutt."

"If you're doing it right it's never that simple." He barrels softly in my ear.

"True." I concede. "Where I come from there are always guys hanging out at all times of the night. This night was no different for me making my way home."

His stroking me becomes much more controlled. The sun and his heat are starting to get to me with the memory of that night and that that happened not too long ago.

"Go on."

"As you can see I'm a nice-size guy."

"A beast," he compliments.

"If I ever have to I can hold my own. But since I was born and bred in the same neighborhood I grew up, and have no beef with anybody, it never had to come to that."

"So you fee safe there?"

"Relatively...from everyone except the police."

"Aren't they there to serve and protect?"

"Some do. Most do more harm than good. Then there is the lame, Andre, who worked the graveyard shift. He doesn't do nothing except sit in his squad car and get off looking at dudes standing on the corner with their pants sagging down."

"Maybe he's patrolling?"

"Hell, no," I say. The roughness of my neighborhood begins seeping out. "Patrolling is patrolling. Sitting there in your squad car with a hard-on admiring is stalking, man. Plain talking. He's done it for as long as I've known him. Got his ass whip over it a few times."

"At least he's persistent." He murmurs low and sexy.

"Now that he can hide behind his badge, he is a fucking untouchable! Licking his chops every time he was something good. Damn near frothing at the mouth when some dude got a dick worth gripping. And it ain't like you can tell that bitch to fuck off."

"Not without trying to put you in handcuffs...though I think that would be a goal."

"Of course," I continue. "It ain't like he wouldn't like to say something too. But seeing that the curfew only applies to those under the age of eighteen, he can't say shit to all these grown men."

"So everyone is at an impasse."

"Exactly. Anyway, between where I have to come from and where I need to go is a thick wooded area."

"A cut?"

"Yeah," I say with his lips now behind my ear. "Because there isn't like a lot of places that are open and nearby, the only place around that Andrew can take his bathroom break is in The Cut."

"I was on my way home when I saw him unzip, taking a leak. I wasn't afraid of him or anything. I just thought I would stay back, do what it do, and proceed after he was done?"

"Why?"

"It isn't like its cool to roll up on somebody taking a piss."

"Is that it? Sounds like there's a back story to me."

"Well, the last time the two of us were face to face was when my boy and I jumped him in the bathroom and used his clothes to sort of kind of sop up the pee around the urinals. He was joned as Piss Boy for a long time. It that never stopped him from doing what he does.

"At any rate," I exhaled with his kisses firm a strong around my collar. "I came across Piss Boy, taking of all things, a piss. When the arch started to trail I thought he was going to bounce back to his car."

"No," he says taking his free hand and begins playing with my nipples.

"No," I breathe. "He started jacking off looking at the fellas under the night."

"Sounds to me like there's no surprise there."

"Not at all. Probably been doing it all along. Probably took the job and the beat because of it. I don't know it was just weird seeing it."

"Violated...makes you feel violated."

I shake my head and speak, "Never that, I just thought since there was another hole in this neighborhood I could fuck. I should've been informed."

He laughs deep but not long.

"Tell me more," he says, moving his playful hand from my pecs to palming my jaw.

"To me at the time, it looks like he was fucking with my way home. So I was piss with that. The way he was jagging off it was more like he was feeling himself rather than busting a nutt.

"It became ridiculous after awhile. So much so that I wasn't even thinking about fucking and I was thinking about popping his lame ass just for the hell of it."

"Watcha do?"

"I started throwing anonymous stuff off the ground at him, thinking he would take his happy-ass and leave. He was a persistent mofo. I waited awhile, and then went over there to him."

Bold." He says with his hand back down over my chest and rubbing my shoulder.

"Nah, it wasn't like I stormed him like when "rapists attack" or something. I pretended like he was just in my way as I quickly I made my way home."

"He must have been startled."

"Of course, more embarrassed than anything else, reaching down and drawing his gun."

"Which one?" He asks jokingly focusing more on my dick.

"The real one. The one he was playing with wasn't even a gun. It was a chopped-ff pencil with something more than a stubby eraser, if you know what I mean?"

"Must've been scared?"

"For a second…but he was too clumsy with it, like Barney Fife. Still, though, I respected the game my hand up in the air because he might be clumsy enough to shoot.

"'Look, man, I was just rolling through from the bus stop home.' I tell him.

"He starts spitting some police mumbo jumbo. Most of it sounded legit, at first, before it started to sound like he was just rambling some nonsense. Like a crazy clueless person. Then, it hit me, after something he said, I can't remember what exactly, but was sort of like a red flag in my head that he was waiting on somebody to roll through. I'm not saying it was me since I wasn't the only one with a late night schedule that came thorough there.

"'C'mon, man'" I say, "'no reason to pull out a gun for the pistol.'

"Instead of calming down, Andre got fired up bitching up something that he wasn't a fag and that he had a girl from around the way. I straight up told him that he was crying like a faggot and the way he was eying dudes hard he was on. Go 'head and admit it.' And lets not forget the proof is in the pudding—his whole life. He threatens to shoot if I didn't 'shut the fuck up.' Even his cussing sounded heavy on the sweet side. I kindly reminded him that if he shout me in The Cut so close to the front where nobody could see us, his little adoring fan club might think it was an attack on them and shot blindly into the woods. Police officer or not.

"If I got shot, I would be nothing more than an unarmed fully-clothed man. If he got shot, he would be an armed police officer with his expose pussy-ass up.

"If you didn't know, I sometimes talk too much. He asked me to raise up out of my clothes. Being at gunpoint, I did. He was supposed to be running the show but he was so mesmerized by the dick, he forgot to think. I didn't even have it up, it was totally calm down by then."

"It hangs quite nicely."

"Like I said before, earlier I thought about riding that ass. So when the mind goes for it, the dick follows."

"Young boys like you go from zero to a hundred with no in between." He says tweaking my nipples again.

"There ain't any other way I know how to do." I say, trying to be hard. "So, I'm looking at him. He's eyeing my dick. I ask him what he wanted to do. His mind is reeling. He wanted to suck some dick. His squad car was across the way, though, and he knew them other fuckers from across the way wasn't above taking the squad car out for a joyride. He wasn't a fag either, so…I told him that playing with my dick wasn't on any fag shit. That in fact in his sworn oath he vowed to protect and serve, and that included my dick."

"He bought that?" He says twisting my nipples hard.

"Not until I told him that the best way to protect it is with his mouth. I didn't think the bitch would buy it but he did. Was on his knees growing and sucking like he was cleaning off a dinosaur bone.

"Andre was so caught up that he didn't even know that I disarmed him until I pulled out of his mouth and forced him face down onto the ground. He was struggling for anything he could get his hands on. Unfortunately, for him, his belt like his pants and underwear were down to his ankles as I creamed at his backdoor."

"That was hot." Arnell says stroking his dick faster between the frictions of my thighs and stroking me off.

"That wasn't the end. I flipped him around because in a pinch cum and spit makes for a great lube."

"You—

"Of course, that was the master plan all along. Right after I figured out that he was waiting on somebody to take him down.

"I pushed through the slimy white foam atop his hole in. It was so soft and wet and slick that it was a little bit made that I wasted my first nutt on trying to make him penetrable.

"So, he on the ground kissing dirt, and I'm on top of him just swimming in it, drowning my dick in his ass. I'm grunting and growling in his ear, telling him that he needs me in him like that. He agreed, begging to me bring, fuck him faster. I fucked him faster, pushing harder with each pistol-cylinder stroke. He's breathing hard one minute and cussing up a storm the other, and riding this carousel back again. He cries that his butt was sore. He said it would be worth the hurt tomorrow because I was putting it down that good."

"I bet you were." He says.

He is still stroking me hard, my balls are clenching upward and that and the violent tweak of my sensitive teats.

"His faggot ass was feeling good to me. I didn't know that once he let go, throwing it back, that it was going to feel like heaven. I was drilling him like I was drilling for oil, digging for gold and mining for diamonds.

"I tell him that I'm about ready to burst. He tells me do what I got to do, as long as I do it deep inside of him. I held him down a little longer than I thought, with his hold talking much smack along the way. It was talking so much smack that I thought the neighbors were going to call the police. I made it submit, though. Shutting it up by loading it with a premium gallon plus."

"Damn."

I try to be as general with telling this story as I can. Reliving every detail in my head put me into another realm. More than I think a major turn-on that has brought me closer to the edge that I thought.

I tilt my head back to rest against his shoulder. He takes his mouth against my neck, his hand against my nipple, and he grips my dick even tighter, knowing my secret as I embrace for the ecstasy that is ready to jut out of my body.

"Ah shit," I suck my teeth, shuttering as my load jets out over the edge.

I am barely able to enjoy my "coming down" before he bends me over and starts going hard underneath my groin. I respect his swagger to let him do this. Let him elude the people that I am his bitch, and that I am taking it even though it is not true.

I am gripping my dick. My hands are stained with my cum. He slams between my thighs like he is in some ass tearing out a new asshole.

His dick feels like fire down there burning tightly pulled up sagging flesh and straggly hairs that is my nutt sac. And the friction between my clamping thigh it brings out grunts and groans that I never knew were possible from a top.

"Aw, fuck," he says pulling me up just in time to watch his dick beneath mine shoot clearly over the edge, disappearing below it hits the ground, about halfway across the middle of the street.

He is exhausted.

I can hear him panting in my ear thanking me. He promises next time we are going to get a room and he is going to help himself to a piece of my hard beautiful ass.

I am fearful at these daring words. I am also calm with his slimy deposits running down my thighs.

He holds me tight.

11:43AM

We collected ourselves, thanking each other and walking downstairs together to the showers.

11:47AM

Afraid to come off desperate by asking him for his number as he's the one that wants to fuck me.

We jump in two adjoining showers; he asks for my name and I ask for him, thought I knew it from earlier.

I knew how and why he isn't going to pursue me. He saw the goods before he got the name.

Damn, I fucked up.

Lesson learned.

Had a good time, but fucked up royally.

I wouldn't be out-of-bounds giving him my info. To do that, though, is to suggest that I would like him to fuck me.

I don't want that, in spite of my attraction to him. I am not ready for that. And to be ready for him, I would have stretch my hole like slutty pussy to be a fraction of accommodating.

11:52AM

I purposely jumped out of the shower first, making sure he sees me as I leave. We give each other lingering glances, wanting to say a whole lot more.

He ignores my childish youth and takes the lead as the mature one, vowing once again that next time the two of us were going to get a room and he was going to fuck me.

"A great top starts off as a good bottom." He yammers on my way to the lockers.

12:01PM

I am dressed and in my car.

12:23PM

At home, and finding the fastest route to my bed.

3:43PM

Wake up from my nap, thinking about the good time I had.

9:05PM

Horny again.
Regret not getting any numbers.
Oh, well, there is always next week.
Oh wait, I forgot about that cute Asian boy from the club. I could give him a call.

BANGERS

"Wait a fucking minute, King, I can't—"

"There's a world of difference between 'I can't' and 'I won't' because there ain't no such word as 'I can't.'" I shot off kindly.

Dame holding his paper cup looked at the warm acrid liquid straight out of my unzipped uncut dick and shook his head.

"Nah, man, I can't." Dame said with his eyes swelling with tears.

"I don't think you heard me, man. I said lap it up!" My voice was simmering with anger, echoing through the storage area of the large warehouse.

"Shit, gulp it down like it's going out of style. Bitch-ass copsuckers know how it do," Kaze, my Chicano piece, grinned showing his grill shinning with platinum and gold and diamond chips.

"King, man," Dame mumbled.

"King is man, all man." I said getting up in his face. "How a homo punk like you walked into this den of men is beyond me. So now that you're ass got caught up in the big leagues, it might behoove you to do what we say…and you better not let a drop come out."

Dame trembled, shaking his head almost violently.

"See, that's the problem," Harlem said, turning his head back. "You're too calm. He thinks he has a motherfucking choice in the matter."

I could see that with three men surrounding him, ready to do whatever, Dame had the sense enough to move the cup closer to his mouth.

There was no room for me, or anybody else to feel sorry for him. This was all of his doing.

"The cooler it gets the harder it is for you to swallow that shit." I said, offering some encouragement.

"Man, I can't."

Dame was like a rat in a cage—no way out. And the thing was it didn't have to be that way. He had several outs and wasn't smart enough to take any of them along the way.

Dame crossed our paths a couple of years ago. He was a friend of a friend that was vouched for to run with our crew. He started off as an errand boy, delivering packages to customers and then moved onto petty selling before earning enough money to buy a whip [car] to become a runner, hauling from Texas to Atlanta up to New England to the various suppliers throughout. He was one of our best. Never ever getting caught. Never even getting so much as a speeding ticket. He had been with us so long and did such good work, we considered him fam.

We thought we were all good until it was brought to our attention that we had a snitch in the midst. It went from Code Orange to Code Red once we discovered that our snitch was an undercover cop. So it was only natural that we started cleaning house, shaking down and roughing up the newbie and those that we thought were soft enough to turn State. We left so much of a blood trail that we thought were going to swim in it. Since we weren't getting answers that way, the traditional way, we started running background checks again.

Surprise, surprise. Our man Dame, the man that we considered blood, no longer existed in the database. We confronted Dame about exactly what happened to his whole identity just falling off the face of this earth. He didn't sugar-coat it, he confessed. He was undercover. The keyword being was, since he had been a defect going on about a year, becoming a friend of the life, fast money and the many benefits that came with it. His superiors were getting frustrated that after all that time; Dame brought them nothing that they could nail us with.

It wouldn't have been such a problem of smoking him, if it wasn't for him being a cop. His title was ex-cop. Nevertheless if word got out about his murder the only thing the precincts would've heard was that he was one of their own.

We had to make him pay, and what a better way to do so than to make him gobble down some of my piss.

"Time is ticking, motherfucker." I said.

"I can't—"

Harlem, with the fury of a volcano blowing its top off erupted with, "I don't want to hear you can't motherfucker. Drink it up!"

Dame swallowed hard, looking for one of us to save him from this hell. But it wasn't like some superhero was going to drop from the sky and rescue him. He got himself in this hell. It was up to him to get out of it.

"I guess my man, Harlem is right. You think I'm playing with your ass. If you don't drink up right now, not only with there be a gut full of piss in your mouth, that cup along with my boys piss will be sliding down your throat.

Damn didn't try to make eye contact. He just looked at the cup with a glass look in his eyes, slowly putting it closer to his lips. And with my help, tipped back his cup.

"There you go. Don't spill a drop." I said, smiling, knowing it was just the beginning.

Once the cup was clear, Kaze came dead out of nowhere and busted him in the jar.

Dame didn't fall. He just toppled to the side, attempting to regain his balance.

"I told you his bitch-ass was a punk." Kaze said, throwing another punch sending Dame in the opposite direction. "Won't ever fight like a motherfucking man."

"That's fine by me. That mean he won't fight for his manhood either." I said throwing his disoriented body over my shoulder after Harlem took his own swing at him. "Watch this."

In one solid stroke, I grabbed the top part of his pants and swiped them down over his ass. He might've been somewhat out of it when the brush of cold air came across him backside as he started flailing and flapping like he was sort of retarded bird trying to fly, with his screams like some kind of crazy-ass mating call.

"What you gonna do bitch." I said, twirling him around like a helicopter, going first one way and then another. "Scream all you want, bitch, nobody can hear you and you're throat is nicely lubed."

As I was spinning Dame about, Harlem and Kaze took turns slapping him about. If I turned one way, one of them would slap him one way and the other the other way. And when I got tired, I threw him up in the air and let him hit the ground in one smooth motion with feet hitting the ground first followed by his face.

"Boom!" Kaze and Harlem howled when his feet gave way underneath him forcing him to land face forward right at my feet.

"I knew your bitch-ass was nasty like that." I snarled.

"So what're we going to do with him?" Harlem asked.

"He just can't say no to putting things in his mouth…" I laughed placing my Timbs on his shoulders, "tells me he probably can't say no to putting other things elsewhere."

I felt Dame struggle to use under my foot, knowing what I had in mind looking at his exposed ass. He tried hard to pull them back up without making it seem so obvious, steadily using the ground beneath him to get them back on.

"I see what you're doing, buddy, might as well part those redbone cheeks and let us do what it do cause we gonna do what it do anyway." Kaze said, laughing along with us.

I released my booth from his shoulder, giving Dame a soft kick in the head. I wanted to remind him that a beat down wasn't out of the cards.

"Raise up, punk!" I commanded. "Raise up!"

Dame was slow to get to his feet, eventually he did though. His lips were busted up, and his nose was bleeding from the few punches that were thrown.

"Stand straight when I'm talking to you."

He worked to stand up straight. He never really did, but ass soon as I thought he had done the best he could do, my heavy first made contact with his jaw.

Dame fell back to the ground.

"The only reason we hadn't taken your bitch ass out to pasture is because only real men deserve to die with honor. Your punk-ass, on the other hand, will go out like a bitch in heat—used and abused!"

I paused. I thought I would give him a chance to say something, fight his way out. Try and claim some shell of his manhood. But without protest, he raised his head up trying to look at us, particularly me, jerking his head over to the wood bench nearby.

It took me a minute to figure out what he was getting to. I told Kaze, who was standing closest to the table to see if there was anything we could "use."

"Oh, man," Kaze grinned. "This fool here got a big–ass bottle of lube over here and like a fucking tower of playing cards.

"For like Strip 'n' Fuck poker." Harlem said.

"Yep," Kaze said, smiling through his words.

"Yo, Har, check his bootyhole." I enlisted.

Harlem knelt behind him. He had to pull his pants down to his ankles to get a hold of his cheeks to take a good look.

"Puckered and tight, but he looks like he been broken in a time or two." Harlem informed.

"No shit." I smirked.

"But then again, greasy pigs usually been hit in the ass before," Harlem said.

"True dat. I think its part of the oath they take. Serve, protect, and give up the booty." I laughed.

"Yeah," Kaze groaned.

"Eh, Kaze," I called out. "Is there anything else over there?"

"Nah, not really. Just this lube."

"What you mean 'nah, not really' that's telling me that there is something else, man."

"Just a bunch of stuff, the keys to his car."

"Oh," I said before being interrupted by…

"Ahhh," coming from Dame.

"Man," Harlem said with his fingers buried deep in his ass. "It feels soft like some good pussy."

"Ahhh, take it out, dude," Dame cried. "I can't take this shit! Ahhh!"

"I know you ain't wincing over some fingers digging your hole when you're your about to be busted wide open by some of the baddest dicks in the game. Last time I checked the three of us were packing double digits."

"Sho' nuff. I know I am. How about you, Kaze?" Harlem asked.

"No doubt, my dick on brick, too," Kaze added.

"Mine, too," I said, rubbing it through my unzipped jeans.

"Shit, you know I've been waiting to get up in that pretty ass since Day One. But *somebody* was trying to put me off talking about 'don't be mixin' business with pleasure." Harlem said.

"Get over it, folk. I didn't know he was a snitch back then. I thought folk was cool. Look at it this way, though, it'll be your pleasure doing it in his business!"

"Yeah," Harlem grinned devilishly.

"Man, stop playing, I can't get down like that." Dame pleaded.

"Ain't this the same dude that said he can't but did?" I asked.

"All the way down to the last motherfucking drop," Harlem said.

"Man, stop acting like such a little bitch." Kaze said.

"He can't help it. He was bred that way." I laughed.

I continued to keep my eye on Harlem steadily fingering Dame, twisting up his face.

"So how that hole feel, man?"

"Like soft butter, baby. I can see us melting up in here all night long."

I whipped out my dick from my pants to show it from all its uncut glory.

"Man, stop fucking around." Dame said nervously. ""None of you get down like that?"

"What part of you trying to fuck us don't you get? We are just returning the favor. You tried to fuck us over. We're going to fuck you."

"Man, please," Dame mustered out below. His mouth hung wide open with silence wincing at the three calloused fingers that Harlem was working him over with.

"I don't see what part you don't get about this going down. I know my boy loves some ass. I think, though, that he wouldn't mess with it unless he was serious about swimming in it."

I pulled my shirt over my head, exposing my ripped body. I went over to Dame and pulled his shirt off too. He tried resisting, but with Harlem playing in his hole it was useless.

"C'mon, man, stop," Dame pleaded one more time.

"That's what you should've done before things got too deep." I said, stripping off my boots and pants.

"Oh, shit," Kaze said astound.

"What?" I said removing the last bit of clothing from my body.

"This dude got handcuffs under all this junk."

"Bring them over." I said, figuring that Kaze had sense enough to bring over the lube. He turned around with nothing more than the handcuffs, I said, "Don't forget the lube, man."

Kaze turned around and grabbed that, with me motioning him to hand it over to Harlem.

"Alright," Harlem perked.

"C'mon, man, please, please," Dame cried, fighting Harlem slapping on the handcuffs.

I reached down and handed my drawers over to Kaze once Harlem had him secure, his hand behind his back with Dame screaming at the top of his lungs. "Kaze, stuff this shit in his mouth so Har don't have his eardrums busted out."

Kaze obliged to a restraining Dame that refused to have his mouth stuffed.

It was a good solid second after that that Harlem was lying on top of him, sinking his greased prick into that hole. Dame was screaming like the bitch I knew he could be as Harlem developed a soulful uptown rhythm.

I allowed Kaze to watch for a minute, to let him get an idea of what he was about to get into. After awhile thought I ordered him down to his knobby knees to work on my piece. Kaze was good at working on a boner, in the front and in the back. The boy drove me crazy by taking these long lingering sniffs in my thick black bush. The musk scent just did something to him as he teased me with these licks at the crease of my legs. I don't know how, but it always made everything else super sensitive. He was merely tonguing my balls and I was like damn. And when he started moving it up the underside to the head, I wasn't ashamed that Kaze had me.

"Hey, Harlem, is that bitch serving it up proper?"

"Oh, yeah," Harlem said wiping the trails of sweat from his face. "Looks like you got a good brain surgeon over there."

"No doubt. His mouth probably feels better than that worn pussy over there." I laughed.

"Shit, it ain't worn. It's like hand in glove, man. Hand in glove."

"Then tear that shit up!"

"No doubt, I got it."

Dame was tearing up from the dick down. He was getting it with Harlem palming his shoulders to get a steady balance. There was no doubt that Dame wanted to let it out, scream at the top of his lungs again but he didn't. Even when Harlem was just straight ramming it into him, rubbing his hole raw.

"Shit, keep that up I'm going to bust one right in your mouth." I said to this twirling thing Kaze was putting on me with his sweet tongue.

"I won't complain, Pa." Kaze said, looking up.

"I know you won't. So calm it down a bit, aiight."

I wasn't down with busting in his mouth, especially not at that moment. I had dreams of releasing a big fat one up the butt of the one that was getting fucked at my feet.

Harlem was pounding him like it was no tomorrow for a good strong while. Dame was letting out sporadic screams in his gaga, begging him to stop.

"Oh, GOT DAMMIT," Harlem bellowed, sinking himself deeper into Dame.

He held his position steady and slowly got up off of him. Dame was lying there with tears streaming down his face, knowing that something wet just filled his guts. But that didn't stop me form telling Kaze to raise up off me and get a helping of his own.

While watching Kaze fucking Dame wasn't as smooth as Harlem, it was just as entertaining with him debating whether he wanted Dame ass up or ass down, changing up every other minute or so.

"Man, what're you looking for?" I asked Harlem wondering about the room.

"Looking for something to wipe my dick with."

"I see a stuffed throat that would be good for that." I said.

"That motherfucker looks like he might bite." Harlem said worriedly.

"No, he won't. His done ass knows he's in some deep shit. He ain't trying to get even more grimy with it."

"You right, shit."

"I know I'm right."

Harlem climbed on the front of Dame, removed his gag, and gave a firm warning to him to 'watch his teeth.'

It wasn't so much that Dame sucked as it was he kept the dick in his mouth while Kaze made up his mind on how he wanted to fuck him. I stayed on the sideline stroking my shit, waiting on my turn to dump my cum inside his sloppy hole. Fuck him over like he almost did me, us.

Even though it looked to me that Kaze was making up shit as he was going along, Dame must've been enjoying because he started throwing it back hard. This, with some dick stuffed in his mouth.

"Oh, shit! I'm going to bust!" Kaze winced, standing steady with cum rushing out of his body.

Kaze was afraid to move, but I moved him out of the way. I knew I was too damn tall to be trying to get down low on the floor. So I picked the fuck up by the handcuffs and tossed him onto the table. Being that I was the third to go, I figured that Harlem and Kaze had worked him nice and loose, at least enough to drive my large member in with the least amount of resistance. But that was a myth, because his walls were choking the hell out of my dick.

"Damn, Dame." I groaned sinking it in deep; pulling it almost all the way out and driving it back in.

I was so busy enjoying the buns and the hard fucking to lend an ear to his useless squealing. Greasy pigs did that. Pigs liked to get poked by pork. I was going balls deep into him, feeling his body trembling like a dangerous earthquake.

"Aw, tell me that shit feel good to you."

Dame was trying to put on a brave front. Unlike Harlem and Kaze, who was fucking him just to get a nutt. I was putting a slow burn on his ass by dicking him down deep, making him appreciate every invading stroke.

"Tell 'em how much you love King inside you. There you go, bitch." I said digging my fingers into his soft flesh going for broke as he whimpered.

I was going to put a hurting on this piece of cop shit. I wanted him to feel me every time his ass sat down over the new few weeks. He must've know exactly what I was thinking, throwing it back every time I tried pulling back.

He wasn't just getting into it. He was always down with the program, keeping the handcuffs and lube at bayside. No. The motherfucker was hoping that if he gave in, threw it back and clamped down on my dick hard that he would eventually have me skeeting like a fire hose.

He was far from making me bust one. He had skills to make me grunt a few out, but I still held the control.

He really started to get into it when Kaze got between his legs and do what he do best. Dame came in no time flat, letting out this satisfying I'm-getting-fucked groan that he couldn't front for. What none of us expected next as that Kaze had went for an instant repeat, using his hands and mouth and had Dame shoot dead on his lips and chin, according to Harlem.

With his asshole gripping like vice now, I was throwing it up in there fast and furiously, pounding out his ass for everything it was worth as he begged me still to take it all out.

"Here it comes, bitch," I mumbled.

And there it was my balls unloading deep in the center of his hole, depositing every last drop before yanking it out.

Instead of just laying there and enjoying what I gave him. He decided to be hardheaded about it, pushing the three loads he received out of his ass. But the joke was on him as it ran down his leg like a runaway river.

"Give me some face, bitch." I said, grabbing his cuffs to grab the back of head to put it in his face.

Damn knew better than to just hold it in his mouth like some clueless punk. He knew he needed to lick it clean, lick the stuff me and my boys had left up in him.

He licked it all up, like a good little pig.

Even though I only fucked him that one, letting Harlem and Kaze go at him like he was their last fuck before the world came to an end, my job was not done…far from it.

After Harlem and Kaze was too spent to move, I was the one that got Dame's car and tossed him in the trunk. And being that I'm so tall and he got one of those tinted window trunks sort of deals, it was sort of hard for me to fit in there with him, spraying him form head to toe in another round of my piss. Harlem and Kaze didn't want to be left out so they followed my lead and stuffed my drawers back in his mouth.

But since the trunk of his car was convenient to the man cab, the sour stench of piss and cum quickly invade my nose as I took the quick drive down to the precinct headquarter to send a message loud and clear, that if they wanted to fuck with us we had no beef fucking the police.

WORKED LOOSE

"How the fuck I know it was you, Sticky Buns?" I smirked, about to give this jaw-dropping motherfucker in front of me the answer to his ever-burning question. "Your scent is like a fucking bakery—I could smell that sweet pop 'n' fresh ass from all the way down the street!"

Although my lowly cocksucker would never come outright and admit it (or maybe *his* sissy ass would), he was wildly turned on by the "compliments" I often gave him whenever his sugar-sweet ass would stop on by. It almost always seemed to tap into his inner 'ho. This in turned brought out his A-Game for whatever perverted or degraded deed I came up with, that day whenever I decided to taunt his tongue with a taste of some of my mean uncut sausage.

The bitch was named Donavon, a naïve piece of shit with wavy dark brown hair on lightly toasted brown skin. I can't even lie; he was a straight-up pretty boy, phyne as fuck, who seemed quite surprised that I opened the door to my apartment butt-ass naked with my Dickies down around my ankles along with my silk boxers—and, of course, with my fat throbbing hard dick kissing the still cool air of the hallway.

"I don't know why you're still on your feet like you're a fucking man. Eyeing me down like you done earned the right to come up from your station in this got-damn world. Like I told your bitch-ass before you're place on this earth is on your knees deepthroating the shit out of my piece."

At first, Donavon didn't finch because I didn't finch. He thought I was playing with his soft crusty ass. When he tried to make his way into my apartment like I usually allowed him to, I still didn't finch, getting the sexy little fuck to get the point.

"You mean, out here out here?" Donavon asked scared and quite shocked. He must've forgot that I was the same dude a week prior that made him drive out to the stadium and suck me off like chrome off of a trailer hitch at a crowded tailgate party.

"Ain't no better place I can think of...unless you want me to start feeding my man to some other dick-starved 'ho?" I said, grabbing at my hard-on for effect.

Donavon took one hard look down at the long narrow hallway where five other apartment doors remained closed. He then looked down the echoing-empty stairwell next to my door before staring at my naked, hard ripped body head-on.

"Time is ticking, man. I can have your replacement here in a minute." I put out there, thinking that it would get the fuck down on his knobby knees.

But, to no avail.

Instead, with his full pink lips pursed, Donavon pleaded, "Shit, can't I do that inside, man?"

"Naw, shawty," I voiced, tapping into my dormant drawl. "I want my dick sucked right out there, right now!"

"What if somebody comes up?" He asked legitimately, looking over the rail, "...or out of their apartment?"

"That's a chance your sweet ass will have to take, sticky buns." I said, watching his light brown eyes light up like a Christmas tree. "Sure, somebody *might* come up the stairs. And sure somebody *might* come out of those apartments, and somebody *might* even discover that you like a big black dick plugging up your pussy-lined throat. Who the fuck said that they might not like it either? But, then, again, getting a taste of some of this chocolaty dick is guaranteed—but like those commercials always say, it's only for a limited time."

Without further ado—just like I knew he would—Donavon sheepishly looked down at my hard dick, pointing dead at him, down the abandoned stairwell and down the lengthy hall before dropping down to his knobby knees. He then cracked open his watery mouth, and took my thick dick down his skinny little windpipe.

If it wasn't for my boy Lo, Donavon and I would have never even bothered crossing paths.

It was only after Lo had landed that good-paying job as a groundskeeper at a local housing project that he came across Donavon's candied-ass and where he lived with his elderly grandmother and baby sister. Over the past few weeks, after that, however, Lo had been trying his damnest to hook up with the pretty little fuck, but had absolutely no luck. So he came up with the next best thing, which was to call in some backup to help claim his prize.

Lo was a very cool guy, but shit-face ugly. He had a huge gash across his face right where the corner of his lips should've ended and his left cheek should have started. All in all, that was merely Strike One against him. And because he was already naturally big and tall like a two-ton silverback gorilla at six-foot-eight, along with the ridiculous amount of muscles we stacked on from our stint in prison, Lo came off much more intimidating than he really was. I was a nice size, too, don't get me wrong. But I had being strikingly handsome well on my side. Put that with the fact that it gave me an exclusive membership to the fantasy league of macho fuckers.

Because of this, after our respective sets had begun to come under siege and come together to fend off the tensions brought on by rival gangs, Lo and I spent a great bit of time shooting the shit by mastering the fine art of flipping guys behind bars. Particularly, those pretty short dudes with those phat juicy asses that were always on their p's and q's, trying hard not to fall into the typical traps of prison life. Once Lo and I agreed on working a particular dude over, I started off on the mark by breaking him down, taking snide little swipes at his fragile manhood, or question thereof that was certain to get into his head and get the best of him when he saw the inner workings of prison life firsthand.

It would seem at first that he would put the idea of two dudes together out of his mind. As it became a constant, however, only one would be a straight-up dude and the other would be his bitch. Then, it would appear that he would have his world and they would have theirs. Amongst the pairings and the brutal rapes, which soon became commonplace behind bars, the guy would come across a unique site: two lifers willing taking turns "taking care" of each other sexually and without bias.

That would get the best of them every time, especially throughout the night when he would only have his thoughts to entertain him.

Give or take a couple of weeks without a good night's sleep, I would see that the mark was no longer on top of his game. I would start engaging him in general conversation to see where his head was at slyly replacing simple words like "brotha" with "baby" and "playboy" with "sweetheart."

When I thought he was letting me get away with that a lot more than I should've, I pushed the envelope a little further by going in for the kill by joking with the other inmates that his "brown eye" felt as good as my girl's good ol' fashioned pussy back home. If he snapped back with something good, it was back to the drawing board. If not, he chose to punk out or storm off like a sissy, he was as good as had. That was where Lo and his ugly scar came in and worked their lovely magic as the understanding confidante. That was where he ran his sweetest game, telling the naïve mark that he knew what it was like to be picked on, especially on the outside, and not having a girlfriend or a prostitute willing to service him much less satisfy any of his sexual needs. And being feared behind bars for being so huge and so intimidating (which he admits had its benefits) often left him friendless except for me, and that was because we went through the fire together.

From there, a friendship was quickly formed with cell drop-bys and tag-along errand runs, followed by an eerily strong bond that could have easily been thinly veiled as a prison marriage without the obligatory sex. After a couple of weeks or more after listening to the heaven and hell screams coming from surrounding cells of inmates having another man inside of them, the mark began to masochistically fantasize about what that must feel like, what it would be like came into mind. Then, after awhile, the mark would look over at Big Lo, feeling like he was the only one in prison that truly understood him. Being that everyone knew by then that the mark was his sidekick the mark also felt that Lo served as his ultimate protector against the rampant attacks he had heard and seen. He would look over at Lo, weighing his options about giving it up to the ugly ogre willingly or risk getting caught up and turned out in some prison hideaway by some prison gangbangers. Before long, Lo got the mark holding his dick and sucking him off, making him spew like a ruptured hydrate. Getting the mark to give up the ass, though, always seemed to be the biggest of all the obstacles. Like sucking dick wasn't really fagging out. Every mark knew that once he crossed that line there was no going back, and it didn't help that it was common knowledge that those that were "flipped" was destined for a prison life of being somebody's bitch—if he got caught doing it. Lo didn't mind, though. He got off on talking to a dude sweetly; convincing him that it was absolutely his choice, whatever that was. Some usually gave it up then and there while others had to think about it for a moment. Some were just plain ol' hardheaded, letting their "great protector" slip away, as the green-eyed monsters of prison got ready to pounce hard. Eventually, they too came around giving up ass like no prison inmate had ever given it up before. After a few test runs, after Lo had worked them loose, he would then share the harvest with the rest of our set and we would in turn claim him as community property, available any time for our convenience.

That was back in prison, of course.

Nowadays, now that Lo and I were upstanding productive members of society, we simply enjoyed the sport of turning out a potential fag. Especially these short pretty dudes with a juicy phat ass much like our boy Donavon.

"So you thinking for yourself now, huh, bitch?" I growled with anger, manically slapping my wet hard dick back and forth across his sweet and sticky bun face.

I was still a bit peeved and turned on at the same time about having to talk that bitch Donavon down to his knees. Peeved that there was even a discussion about it, and turned on to the fact that in spite of his better judgment and understandable concern and fears, he was still game to do anything to get his mouth around my dick.

When I plugged my dick back into his mouth, he seemed quite sated using his slick tonsils to ease me further down his throat. I gripped the sides of his face and ears, steady moving my dick in and out of his mouth. Just when I thought I was the master of his oral domain, the dirty bastard started to do something with the back of his tongue that literally had me one good stroke from just letting loose down his throat.

And I couldn't have that—not at his will.

So as I felt the sharp bristles of his shaped goatee scrape against my hairy balls, I took one firm hand to the back of his hooked head, and forced him down on my dick.

He gurgled and choked, gagged and cooed, and frankly loved every minute of it.

"Yeah, bitch, I got that throat wide open now, like you my proper bitch," I said, letting my baritone voice carry down the hall and down the stairwell.

Even if I didn't know that every one of my neighbors that lived on my floor was gone to work, I still wouldn't have given a damn. Taking some solace in the fact that I could feel his asshole twitching from all the way up in his mouth.

My dick was raging mad at the mere thought of this, and my husky orbs were ready to burst out of control. I had to do everything in my power just to hold back, just a little while longer. His mouth was feeling just that good. The only choice I had in my arsenal was to pump my dick in his mouth piston-style.

I was in the zone. I could feel my dick swell threefold in his tightening mouth. Like I, he knew exactly what was coming and tried his best to pull off. But I wasn't having that, reminding him that the courteous thing for me to do was let him receive the fruits of his labor.

"Stay still and swallow hard, or I'll take it out on that sweet ass of yours, Sticky Buns."

That just seemed to do it for him. Tapping into his inner 'ho, his throat relaxed without protest, allowing even more of my dick into his mouth. Of course, my victory was short-lived when I let out a budding groan and flooded his wet mouth with my warm sticky cum that he soon took down the pipe like the cum-thirsty 'ho he was meant to be.

It took awhile. But once I felt that I was completely drained, I pulled him off of my dick and shook it off across his ever-loving face.

"Next time," I said, catching my breath, and pointing my finger at him, "I tell your pop 'n' fresh ass to do something, I expect you to do it with no sass. You hear me? When I whip out my man, your knees better hit the ground running, mouth open ready to receive, and cum ready to gulp down like it's your favorite cherry-flavored slurpie. 'cause next time you ain't actin' right you getting any of this," grabbing my dick and rubbing the wetness across his face one more good time.

With that off of my chest, I took a real good look at the poor sap. Looking like his mouth needed to snap back in place with it looking like it was desperately hoping for another round of dick. Rather than ruin the moment with meaningless words, I simply stepped back from the threshold and slammed the door in his sugar-sweet face.

"Eh, Lo," I smiled into the phone, doing up my Dickies, and making my way to my computer desk. "There ain't a damn thing that bitch won't do for a dick. I know without a doubt now that before we can take shit to the next level I got to tap that ass. Shit, that motherfucker is ripe and ready for his shit to be turned out and then some. Let me tell you what I had the boy do all this week! Let me just start off with what I did to the worthless fuck just five minutes ago...

...

From my angle, Donavon was a simple kid to figure out. He was one of those kids who was forced his nose to the grindstone because it was more important that he carried the well-wishers of his struggling community on his back rather than be allow to have a little fun. Unfortunately for him, though, it bred his hankering for a taste of the wild side, believing that having some raunchy bottom bitch by his side was the end of all ends. And it was—for awhile. Particularly during his senior year of high school when he had made all of his credits and the only thing he had to do was sit around until graduation.

And soon it came, his high school graduation and his eighteenth birthday.

Aside from still having to live with his nagging grandmother and his baby sister to keep down expenses, Donavon was ready to get his grown man on, which in his world pretty much meant spending the whole summer throwing some dick in his broad and getting everything ready for college.

Then, one late summer night as he made his way through the cut after another nice day of swimming in some pussy, he saw something that would just forever fuck with his head. Something that he didn't even know was an option on the table.

While Donavon was pretty much cool with everybody at school and in his 'hood, there were at least three dudes that he simply tiptoed around at any given moment what he had told me from earlier conversations, the three dudes were allegedly a buck wild bunch of hardcore thugs, known to pounce on anyone, male or female, for even looking at them crooked. There was even one incident that even Lo had filled me in on when he saw one of the three duded who had came across a recently-released inmate that apparently still had some debt lingering over his head before he went in. And how the story went, the dude snatched off his belt, somehow got the bastard crawling around on his hands and knees, and started beating him silly, going up and down the street and back again. "My boss man then had the nerve to ask me, 'how come I didn't step in?'", Lo told me one night over some beers. "I wanted to tell the shit, he didn't pay me enough. But I played it off square, telling my boss that I didn't dabble in domestic quarrels anymore." As Lo hinted around the real reason of how he got caught up in the system in the first place: defending a toothless 'ho that wouldn't give him the time of day from her ass-whuppin' pimp, who got her to flip the script on Lo once the police arrived.

Anyway, according to Donavon, the three dudes and their reputations had begun to reach a fever pitch that summer when deserving bodies were hitting the ground from stray bullets that came from anonymous guns in and around their housing projects. The more that happened the more their faces became littered with teardrop tattoos, suggesting that they were the ones behind the murders. Though, whenever any of the three saw Donavon, they always managed to give him a head nod and what sometimes looked like a devilish smirk. So it came as quite a blow to his thought process that night when he saw all three of them in the cut getting blowjobs by this known fag called Desirae.

"He was bobbin' his head up and down those piles of dicks like it was nothing," Donavon confessed to me over a midnight snack one time.

He was blown away. Not at the fact that sissies sucked dick, but men at the epitome of macho-ness in the 'hood would allow such an effeminate creature to even touch their manhood like that. I could have went in and dropped some prison science on him, telling him in many cases that was the greatest sign of respect from a fag was when he kept his head down, spoke when he was spoken to, and serviced a dick on wordless command.

Nevertheless, Donavon was intrigued when the three dudes clowned Desirae by letting go of three simultaneous nutts dead in his face, as Donavon watched from afar. As the days progressed, Donavon came across Desirae in the cut sucking off everyone from the old gray-headed dude to the sixth-tier drug dealer with a wife and two known girlfriends. Even Lo had to admit to getting some of that throat.

Donavon was too scared to get in on the action, so Desirae caught up to him one night in passing. That was the night that Donavon found out that a dude could give better head than some girls.

But that was just only the beginning.

Desirae had some friends that would not only give him head anytime he wanted it, but would get on their hands and knees and offer up their greased booties, squealing and hollering about his big dick. This only put Donavon on the onramp of being turned out, when one night some anonymous thug from somewhere around his neighborhood came up from behind him, nearly scaring the living shit out of him and his new swagger. Of course, the dude was only mistaken, thinking that Donavon was an old friend trying to skip out on a gambling debt. Even so, Donavon told me, he never knew that his dick could get so hard with another dude pressed up so close against him like that.

A few days later, Donavon thought he caught the wandering eye of some of the other neighborhood thugs. Unlike before, though, when he came through the cut with his mind on dinner, he started wondering if those thugs were thinking what he was thinking about as he arched his back to the ceiling, spanking his monkey and started to play with the tender skin near his tight booty hole, dreaming about those sexy-thuggish motherfuckers taking their time turning him into their bitch in a gangbang fantasy-style setting.

He couldn't go there, he remembered, calming down after most of his powerful nutt to date sailed across the room taking out some of his beloved posters. Those were dudes he grew up looking up to, went to school with. Sure, some of them he only knew in passing. Still, though, even if he had a chance to give it up to just one of those dudes, life would be like the cherry on top of a hellhole sundae, with news about the quite little light-skinned boy that hopped off the bus every single afternoon coming from school to fag out for all those motherfucking thugs, and having that reoccurring dream of having to fight those thugs baby's mommas' over the rights to their dicks.

Poor Donavon could not be obvious to the fact that his glances at just one of those gorgeous men was just a lot longer than they should have been, the way he covered his hard piece of equipment with his books said it all to my boy Lo.

Donavon was grown enough to be out of high school yet young enough to be dumb and dickstruck, Lo told me the night he unveiled his master plan to help turn Donavon out.

Best of all, coming somewhere out of left field, we came across the unbeknownst information that while Donavon may have sucked dick he was definitely a bona fide backend virgin. Something that I found to be tried and true the second time my ten-inch dick pacified the natural-born cocksucker's mouth when I took it upon myself to rub my rough and heavy mitts down his ass crack. His hole was so small and so tight that he damn near broke off my pinky finger passed the first knuckle.

In spite of my sadistic flare, I never again tried fingering him, letting him become his own slave to the "what if" feeling of having his ass played with as he feverishly worked over my dick.

I knew that the "what ifs" had finally started to get the best of him when he told me about the night he saw the three dudes running a train on Desirae and the way he was loving it. So much so that someone had to stuff a bandana in his mouth to keep down the excitement. Given the fact that Donavon had sucked me off in places he had never even dreamed of, he summoned the courage to call me up a few days after the hallway incident, that his folks were headed out of town for the weekend, and he wouldn't put up "too much of a fuss" if I happened to stop on by and kicked it with him one day.

Not a man usually up for subtleties, I told Donavon straight-up that I wouldn't mind rolling though, but only if he was game about letting me be the first to tag that ass. He hesitated for a minute. It wasn't because he was scared or anything like that. He had thought it through before he even picked up the phone. He hesitated because he wanted to come off coy, making me promise to be gentle with him "if" we got down to business.

Friday night rolled around, and I pulled into a small crowded parking lot littered with some downright gorgeous thugs and fugly (fuck-ugly) looking slugs standing around. I gave the liquored group a nod out of respect, stopping short of coming out of my skin to holler at this short Boricua-looking boy with a shaven bald head and an oh-so-damn! phyne phat juicy booty that looked like it could crush steel poles for months. But, I digressed, going about my business as I remember verbatim everything Donavon told me about going around the corner of the third building to the left and reading up the stairs to the door on the right.

The freak inside of me wanted to shuck off my pants when I got to his door. Common sense kicked in and told me not to go there. Not yet. Just in case by a small chance I had the wrong door.

I knocked.

Donavon opened it, like I expected, standing there shirtless, showing off his lean muscles wrapped tightly around his skinny frame, and causually invited me in.

He stared at me hard.

"What?" I finally asked him, pulling my shirt over my head, letting him love the huge rock-solid prison muscle that still covered my body.

He smile ran a mile wide, pushing the door closed behind me.

"I just thought you're freaky-ass would've been at the door with that fat knob hanging out of your pants.

"Would've," I smirked, taking full note that his nice body was only complimentary to his good-looking mug. "But seeing all these hoochies around there, I was afraid one might take a look at the stick and would've tried to rape me. With all the shit I got going on I don't need to be some crumbsnatcher's daddy."

He laughed, making me forget my main focus with his naturally perfect set of teeth. I moved in closer in on him, and for the first time in our depraved relationship I went in for a kiss. As my tongue made its way down his startled mouth, I quickly snapped back into play, reminded that it was all about running game and plucking ass so that me and Lo could have access to something when the well ran low. And for effect, I straddled him to my waist like an absent lover and slammed him to a piece of his grandmother's wall free of framed mementos.

I came in with the full intent of playing him like a fiddle. So I did, dry humping him eagerly against the wall. I felt his nature rise instantly as I took my time to leave hickeys across his neck. I took it a step further, stuffing my hands down in his jeans and cupping his virgin ass. I knew that if this was going to go off without a hitch, I needed him hot and horny ass hell, begging for it like a crack fiend.

He failed not to disappoint directing me to his bedroom.

He flipped on the switch upon entering; loving every passion mark as I quickly laid him down on the bed. He sort of got me by locking his legs around me, but fumbled horribly by trying to shuck off his long shorts after putting me in a vice grip.

"Trying to put the chicken before the egg, ain'tcha shawty," I said, raising off of him and sliding off his shorts and underwear.

"I just want to please you, Pa." Donavon cooed so sexily, opening up my belt for me.

He didn't even wait for my dick to greet him. He just went for the kill, pulling it through the slit of my boxers.

"Damn, shawty," I smiled, looking down at him, palming my swollen manhood. "Look at you, gripping the dick like you got papers on it."

"I do." Donavon winked, jutting his tongue out at my dick.

He was soon leaning forward, bathing it in warm spit and coning his tongue to work my shaft overtime, working hard just to make me want to leak just a little.

"Shit, keep on working that tongue like that, Sticky Buns, and I might just have to sign on the dotted line." I lied, with a hint of sincerity.

He worked his tongue into my piss slip, loving the "compliment" nevertheless as he found a new vigor breathed into his lungs.

"Shit, keep on doing that and I'm going to have to bust an ol' fashioned nutt off in you're mouth." I said, feeling my balls coming to a boil. "I came here to bless that tight booty, aiight."

He then started slow bobbing, thinking that he was still keeping me entertained all the while preventing me from skeeting a load down his throat. As it seemed, however, his slow bob was about to sink me into deep trouble.

"Enough dick for you!" I joked, making a play on a sitcom I saw, popping it out of his mouth.

I stepped out of my pants and boxers, and took out the condom and lube.

"Damn, Bossman pulled out a black condom out on me," he laughed nervously as I slipped them on.

"Yeah," I smirked, "thought I would throw it on for the special occasion that your bitch-ass didn't *punk* out."

I kept on looking at him, wondering what was going through his pretty little head. Was he game? Was he scared as shit? What?

Donavon just looked up at me, like he knew what was going on in my mind, and responded with, "I'm ready to go all the way. But like I said, I never had anybody in me like that before."

"So?" I said, trying to come off harder than hard.

Even though I had a great plan worked out in my mind, he could see that I did give a little bit of a damn about popping his cherry.

"So?! I'm scared as fuck!"

"Don't be." I assured him like I knew. All I saw was that I was getting some virgin-tight booty. "Relax that juicy little ass of yours and don't fight it, and you should be good."

"I bet that is what you say to all of them." He joked nervously.

"Naw," I said, looking down at him, and saw every kind of emotion run through his head. He was committed yet scared out of his fucking mind looking over at my black-covered, big black dick wishing that it didn't live up to the typical stereotype.

"I ain't going to hurt you." I said sincerely.

I wasn't getting all lovie-dubie, but I saw that it was something he needed to hear and something he needed to believe in.

He turned around, and presented his bubble ass to me. The only thing that would have made it more beautiful was if he had oiled it up, giving it a nice sheen, a nice shine. As I spread his mounds, I saw that tight little buttonhole butthole in the off-center area of his ass crack putting into perspective that punching a dick deep down through was really nothing more than a brilliant idea up until that point. At least, I thought, I could make the point of no return more enjoyable.

"Turn that ass around." I said injecting a bit of bass and sex into my voice.

Like a good soldier, Donavon turned around.

I snatched him up to his feet.

"Trust and believe, when I'm busting open that cherry I promise you that I will be watching all of those beautiful sex faces." I added, pulling him in close.

He was ready, but tense. That only seemed to melt away when I started playing with his hard pointy nipples.

After awhile though, Donavon took the initiative and pulled me on top of him onto the bed, letting me lie down beside him and slowly finger his hole as he let out wild gasps and moans. "Damn, baby," I grinned and kissed. He was no doubt relaxed, but his hole would not let up even as I tried to work more globs of lube into his hole. I mean, I did everything to work that sucker loose from massaging it to stretching it open.

No luck.

In a twist of events, however, while I wasn't making any leeway, Donavon was giving off subtle hints that he was ready to get fucked. That was until he came outright and said it. "Damn, boy, I need your man up in me."

That was enough for me. Fuck all the niceties, I thought, sliding him to the edge of the bed.

I aligned my dick with his virgin hole. As I rubbed it in to get it through, his hole only sucked in part of the tip as if to say some shit in broken English like "too big, only room enough to slip in a toe". I thought at first that I would roll with the punches because he was a stone cold virgin, and before I did anything I needed him to relax just a little bit. I mean, I had been in predicaments that took forever to work my way inside of a dude. Many of them weren't even virgins any more. This, however, was ridiculous. It was like forever on top of forever. When I decided to just try to go in for the kill, his closed slit decided to take a different take.

While my main concern then was about breaking in the rest of his stubborn seal, Donavon was moaning and groaning like he was getting the dick down of his life. Not as if he was getting bitched out and screwed but as if he was happy that he finally got some dick to touch his closemouthed bootyhole.

"Man," I griped. "You got a deadbolt on that ass. I can't even get the head in right. I might have to call in back up."

Donavon was acting like he was in Seventh Heaven grinding his taunting hole against my dick.

"If I can barely get one up in me, what make you think two is going to work?" Donavon wringed.

"Oh, you'll see." I said, reaching for his cell phone nearby.

About ten minutes later, Lo pooped up at the door. Due to his lowly position barely paying enough to keep him a place nearby, his boss man got him a rent-free apartment on the premises, which kind of spooked Donavon as he opened the door for the big man.

"Remember me, folk?" Lo and his belly-driven bass carried throughout the small apartment.

"Let him in," I said, from my position in his bedroom doorway.

Lo came in followed by Donavon, looking as if he just knew he had bit off a bit more than he could chew.

"Don't worry." I answered the thoughts reeling through his trembling body. "I'm going to get him to lay on the bed while you treat him to that First Class Head like you do, and I'll play with that cockteasin' booty of yours."

A man of my word, I stuffed my face between his cheeks and heard the slurps of a young buck blowing off a man packing a bull-hung like he had been doing it for centuries. Lucky for me, though, great head was like kryptonite to Lo, and before someone like Rachael Ray could say "parmesan reggiano," Donavon was fighting with all the thick cum clogging up his digestive tract. And as he was gasping for air, I ran my pipe up in his helpless hole like a train coming at full speed.

"Ah, stuck you in the ass," I crooned, listening to him trying to scream out with plenty of cum blocking his throat with a lot of the milky substance landing on Lo's flat stomach. "Didn't anybody tell your sweet ass not to fuck with an anaconda…he might not be alone."

I was a bit thrown that once I was able to put it up in that ass, I was in there.

After a few rough and rhythmic thrusts delivered straight to his man-spot, Donavon nutted like a fool on the sheets below him with no assist. No hands. But that had absolutely nothing to do with me as I went to work on that juicy phat ass of his.

"Let me get some of that ass." Lo said some time later when his dick came back to life.

Lo was sitting on the edge of the bed while our piece of ass creamed to the high heavens all into the pillows beneath him.

"Cool," I said, supplying another ball-deep thrust. "I got this shit worked loose now."

"Like a 747?" He said, referring to an inside joke.

"Yeah," I grinned.

Once I got in a few more wicked knee-deep burying lunges, Lo and I traded places as I took my new place in front of Donavon on the bed, pulling his face out of the pillow and wincing like a motherfucker when Lo slid his man up in him.

"Told you, I was going to watch those sex faces," I said, making him take an unwilling lick of his own cherry juice before snatching off my empty condom.

Donavon looked like he wanted to say something real bad, but it appeared that he had so much pain up in his ass that it left the poor boy speechless. The next thing I know, I hear something sounding like a water gun going off. Before I realized it, it was Donavon letting go of another nutt with no assist, with droplets splashing off of the bed and onto my legs. I guess that must have been enough to send my boy Lo completely over the edge, going from jackhammering that sloppy second hole to letting out a mighty roar, holding the body steady at the hips as he damn near blew Donavon right into me and my still-standing proud dick.

"Man, was it worth it?" I asked Lo with his eyes screwed shut.

"Shit, yeah," Lo exhausted a full two minutes later, disengaging from Donavon, who was crying big deep sobs. I could only imagine his hole being packed to the brim by a man infamously known for his gallon-size wad of cum. "The only thing that would've made it better was if I could've said I had first-tagging rights."

"You set me up?" Donavon said in wondrous disbelieve when his voice came back to.

"Folk, please, I used to be in prison. All I did was pluck phat booty with or without the consent of the owner."

Donavon looked up at me, and gave me a smirk that only a deflowered virgin could. "The joke's on you, though. After watching all those man-on-man flicks, I really wanted to be turned out by more than one hardcore thug. If I was going to give it up like a punk, why not be put out of commission like a fucking fag?"

"You're absolutely right," I beamed calmly, giving him his props for having heart as I smacked my still-full, hard-on against his chin. "I hate to break it to your wish-listing ass, but the joke is really on you. Eh, Lo? What becomes of the virgin boy with the juicy phat ass when left alone with two big, big-dick horny ex-cons for the weekend?"

"Weekend?" He mouthed silently scared, obviously not getting the memo that we weren't the kind of "gentlemen" to just hit it and quit it.

"Become a certified cum slut?" Lo asked.

"No," I said, chuckling. "That's a given. Try again."

"Hope and pray that he could hold in his shit after we're done?"

"Close," I said. "The answer the judges were looking for was 'He will be lucky if he could sit or stand upright by Thursday of next week."

"Thursday of next week," Lo repeated softly, rubbing his dripping dick on some dry part of Donavon's ass.

■■■

It should really go without saying that we spent the entire weekend screwing like cats and dogs, practically treating every passing hour like it was our fucking last. Then, on top of that, Lo and I was having the time of our lives when neither one of our big dicks refused to die down in the spirit of depraved competition, dumping load after draining load in some orifice that the other wasn't occupying at the time.

Lo and I were quite proud of ourselves, turning him from a curious virgin bottom to a full-fledge houseboy treating us to deep-tissue massages and taking our food orders between trysts of carnal and sleeping pleasures.

Unfortunately, the weekend could have ended on a much higher note, if it hadn't been for Lo wanting to air out the stuffy room from the staunch stench of feet and ass. Being that it was late and his grandma was way overdue, and being that the apartment was on the second floor, I thought it would be fun to crank out my final nutt by fucking our "used" house bitch out of the wide open window.

Everything was good.

I was shoving everything I had in me into his battered butthole trying to get him with due diligence to get him to give up his recent vow of stubborn silence. I wanted him to let the empty parking lot below know how good he was getting dicked down. He was being hardheaded, grabbing onto the brick exterior.

I thought I had all the time in the world, so I didn't mind. That was until I saw some headlights in the distance turn into the entrance of the housing projects, making its way towards the parking lot.

Oh shit, I thought.

He must've seen it too because he started letting out a deep sighs as I bucked against him harder and faster, stammering stammer like he caught a case of Tourettes syndrome and wasn't missing any of the cuss words.

"I'm almost there, baby," I said, looking at the car turning into the parking lot. "Shit, now or never."

I drove it in deep, spearing him for all that it was worth, and soon splattered his guts with what was left of my sputtering nutt. He, in turn, let out a loud betraying cry just as four men got out of the car and happened to look up at us; more at him since he was the one hanging out of the window.

Lo, who was standing nearby, told me to hold him still.

Not knowing what to expect, I did what I was told and held him steady out of the window while Donavon tried hard to work his way back in.

Lo grabbed the window and pushed it all the way down on him.

It wasn't like hurting him or anything, but being that Donavon kept his hands outside of the windowsill, it made it very hard to open it from his angel. And with him making such a huge fuss over it, it only drew a lot of unwanted attention to himself.

"Put you're clothes on!" Lo shouted, already clothed and throwing on his size nineteen boots.

By the time I got my head wrapped around what was going on, I was out in the parking lot net to Lo standing face to face with the four men, one of whom was definitely a sissy with processed hair.

"'member how you said we set you up?" Lo shouted up to Donavon still struggling to get the window open. "Think off this as the sequel."

Huh?

"We left the door wide open for ya to go get some." Lo said to the men.

Three of the dudes gave a hard head nod and headed back around the corner of the building from where we came from. Lo walked the sissy over to another building. I took my lonesomeness as a cue to get in my car to go home with Donavon hanging out of the window cussing up a storm, trying to get unstuck.

■■■

Days later, Lo called me up and told me about what unfolded after we left. Which by that point wasn't hard to piece together being that I stuck around long enough to listen to Donavon hollered to the heavens as his body roughly bobbed back and forth out of the window. Except the part that his grandmother came home the next morning to find her only grandson, the pride of the community, hanging out of the window butt-naked with his slutty butt iced in dried cum.

Shortly after that he was put out of his apartment, and became good friends with Desirae, and the two of them became community property for the bad boys of the projects.

MARRIED TO THE GAME

The funniest thing was that I thought I was going to be the first to lure in some poor unsuspecting woman down the aisle and then cheat on her left and right. Of course, I was planning on being a gentleman about it, being discreet—at first—before becoming sloppy with my actions and eventually setting the tone to strut down to the courthouse to file for a divorce.

I always pictured my friend Mitch being the first to pop out of the closet in his motorcycle leather and vogue-ing his way down to the nearest gay parade route. The come-across straight-acting fuck had been married before. The first marriage was a charade and really didn't count. She was a stern racist carpet muncher posing as a carefree fag hag with her eyes steadily on her provisional trust fund. But here he was, the furry fuck, getting married again. Not only was he putting himself in the line of fire, he was doing it again with another woman.

The major difference between the two wives was that his newest one was a heterosexual woman.

To put it plainly, as for it to not to be a complete understatement, his new wife Meghan was a complete nymphomaniac.

First off, it isn't slander if it is true. And it very much was when it came to her.

Secondly, I would be lying if I said the girl didn't have any charm behind bleach-blond mane. She had the allure of a rural girl fresh off the farm with naïve goals of making it big in the city.

Although I was good friends with Mitch, I never told him that I met his soon-to-be wife first. In fact, neither of them knew each other at the time. I met one because of the other.

Meghan was one of those freaky white girls that shamelessly strolling down the aisles of Wal-Mart hungry for some "colored" dick. Black. Brown. Red. Yellow. It didn't make much of a difference. And to top it off, she was like that potato chip commercial from back in the day, she couldn't just have one. Two or more was the standard.

This was how I met her, flashing her pink panties to me and my boy Paco. Next thing I know, we're at somebody's crib. Paco had her pussy, I was digging in her ass, and she was alternating back and forth between these two other dudes giving head.

I knew she wasn't a virgin to get hemmed up like that, but it wasn't long before I came across her tag as the "Super Store Slut." She was so well used by the men in the community that they pledge to pitch in to get her tubes tied. Because heaven forbid if she ever got knocked up! She may not be able to tell Maury who the father of her baby could possibly be, but she could tell whose dick belonged to whom in a blind taste and feel test.

I don't ever think she was "turned out" per se, based on prior experience. I just think she was told by her ultra conservative Rebel-flag redneck parent to stay in her lane and stick within her white race. Even though she was known to take on big-dick white studs, she had a little rebel of her own ser own serving up all the other racial colors of the rainbow.

Mitch was different.

He was a straight-laced motorcycle-loving dude that once had it all. Back then, his interaction with other races were either from afar, if not far and few between. But that had more to do with his social circles than anything else. That all changed when he got greedy and got his ass sent to prison. He admitted that he was sort of glad he got sent up the river. He always thought he was a fag, and naively thought prison would be a place to quench his curiosity without repercussion. Fortunately for Ron, he wasn't "initiated" into prison with four or five guys on his back. He was taken in by this big black guy that made him his prison wife. From what he told me, they had a "marriage" with plenty of sex, clearing up years of sexual questioning. Halfway through Ron's Sentence, his prison husband died of a massive heart attack. He wasn't even allowed but a minute to grieve before a prison gang stormed his cell and ran a train on him. Instead of being the worst thing in his life, he found it quite calming after such a tragedy that so many men wanted to share the same hole his husband had for so many years.

He assumed that after they had had him that he would be passed off some low-wrung gangbanger. To his surprise, he was kept as the "house bitch" for the entire gang, forced to wear butt-hugging Tidy Whites until someone decided he needed to dye them all pink, making them out to be makeshift panties.

Ron said that the second half of his sentence was blur after that. He was passed around so frequently that it practically ate up all of his time.

Once he was released, he went through withdrawal. He was fienin' for it like crack to a crackhead. But there was hardly any place to feed the need except to travel out forty miles to the Rest Area at night and suck off the horny truckers. It offered a mild fix. His appetite however was for black dick, something of his neck of the woods.

So he moved, landing a job as a foreman to an all-black staff, with my boy Kirk who was one of his subordinates. He used to tell me all the time that something was up with his boss man. He couldn't put it into words, except that he always kept one of his black male employees in his office. He never really wanted anything other than to talk, and hint around about the curious sex lives of his employees.

One night my other boy Gary and I was horny as hell when we came across this number to this chatline strictly for man-and-woman hookups. We thought we might come across a woman that would do us in a threesome. At the time, we were looking for born-ready women, so of course the line was littered with pre-pot transsexuals on the women's side. So as we scanned through the messages hoping to luck up on some freaky women, we came across this message from this baritone-based country bumpkin talking about strutting around in some women's panties, being a whore for black cock. The way the guy's voice contradicted what was willing to do was something that intrigued me. Seeing that my friend claimed to be 100% hetero, I was ready to pass it on up until Gary mentioned he was interested in seeing this, too.

So after a little back and forth, he gave us his number and we drove over to his crib. It was so littered with motorcycle and parts that we thought we were led on a wild goose chase. We were tempted to turn back, but something in us just said ring the doorbell. And to our disbelief, we were at the right door with this furry redheaded fuck parading around in some pink see-through panties.

He offered us a seat on his sofa along with some Coronas and sucked us off as we gulped our beers down. He was slightly teed that we didn't play with his panties or hairy ass. But being that we were black and vowing to comeback, he rode his black dildo in anticipation. I knew that after Ron sucked us off a few times that Gary wasn't going to venture beyond the typical blowjob. So I made it my sole duty to please his booty, toying with it for a few days before making that plunge in it.

He turned into a total bitch in heat after that. Anytime my dick thought about getting hard around him, it was down his throat or up his candy ass with no questioned asked. I guess my lust for him and his eager ass began to eat into my time with my friend because they were getting concerned about my after-work disappearing act.

After a couple of more weeks, I let a couple of my friends in on the secret, taking turns fucking him. It soon started to look like one of those black gangbang pornos with that token white bottom taking miles of dick in every hole.

Between bouts of sex, the tow of us became oddly endearing friends. I was the best man during his first wedding, and tried to have his back the moment he professed he was going to live life as an openly gym man that loved black dick.

I assumed things were going to plan until he informed us after one of our weekly get-togethers that he was getting married again. And when we found out that it was to Meghan, a chick that we all banged and in some cases was still banging, we had the decency not to laugh in his face, knowing that she was trying to clean up her reputation and that he wasn't exactly out. Most importantly, after the vows were said that one of them was going to give up the drawers.

It was in their nature.

Barely a month after their wedding, I led two of my fellas over to their house to start some trouble. I thought if we could get the two of them together, air open there past and resume our fucking. What hadn't come across our mind (but should've) was to only find one of them at home. Somewhat of an added bonus, if we could get a nutt before the other spouse returned home.

Meghan practically led us from the front door to the back, stripping her clothes off as we followed behind her. The only thing she kept on were her pink panties as she fought to take each of us in her mouth, palming the other two in her hands.

It was like old times, watching her handling dick like she was a juggler. She was doing such an excellent job that nobody bothered to reminder her that she vowed to change her ways after she got married.

"Get my dick nice and wet, bitch!"

"Suck it, yeah!"

"She's swallowing that shit."

"I bet that pussy is fired up!"

"Waiting on some dicks to run up in it!"

These were just a few of the things said before I took a seat in the recliner in the corner and lubed up while the two of them picked her up off the floor and impaled her on my dick. For a newlywed she was unreasonably tight, tighter than she was before. I handed off some lube to one of my fellas as she eased his dick into her ass.

She was being stuffed to the brim with my other boy, filling her mouth.

We went at her a good little while as my fellas switched places, taking turns in her ass and muffling the yelps wanting to escape out of her mouth.

It took everybody by surprise—even me—that I was the one to come first. She was too damn tight to hang. She must have been tight in other places, too. My boy in her ass was stammering as he broke a load off in her ass while the other one flooded her throat.

"Don't be spillin' them dead babies on me." I said to her, watching the cum foam out of her mouth.

While this was going on, we heard what sounded like a soft funny sneeze come from the closet.

"What the fuck?"

I scooted Meghan up off of me and investigate what is going on in the closet.

My boy beat me to the punch to find Ron in the closet with nothing on but his pink panties.

I thought at first that this was some sort of planned shit. Like she would do all and he would watch from a distance. The shock on her face and the hurt in his eyes said it all.

"I don't know why either of you look so devastated," I said. "She's a slut and he's a dick-lover."

I instructed Meghan to get on the bed. I told Ron to go over there and kiss her on the mouth and fish out as much cum as he could. He was then instructed to eat out our other deposits left in her cunt and ass.

He lapped it up like a kitten to a bowl of milk while we stood around looking on and laughing up a storm. Calling him every name but the one he was born with. I took a seat back in the chair, letting the fellas pushed him out of the way.

Watching them taking turns to do her again, got me excited all over again. Ron was standing around in his panties looking like a lost cause.

"Bring your ass over here." I finally barked.

He tried to put on a front, acting all hesitant. I broke the ice by shouting at his wife, shouting obscenities from her fucking, about how her new hubby took dick better than she ever did. She was too caught up to respond. That didn't stop me from telling tidbits about our past rendezvous. Telling the room about the time we took Ron and his panties to a motel room where we filled him up with Vaseline and fucked the night away.

I could tell by the look in his eyes that Ron remembered the night quite well too. He was getting excited about it. He knew that the only way to quench his thirst was to open up his mouth and take as much of it as he could.

"See, I knew you ass wasn't use to drinking secondhand cum. You get your shit straight form the tap!"

I was just what he needed to hear, attempting to suck the life out of my dick. Whether Meghan heard me or not when I put Ron's business out there, I thought it was only fair to tell some of hers. Telling him about the time we filled several shot glasses of cum mixed it with rum and challenged her to drink it up. She downed fifteen shot with an average of four loads a shot, she gulped down a lot.

Meghan was on the bed enjoying her orgasm helping my friends do the same. All the grunting got the best of me, and before I knew it I was skeeting a load down Ron's throat while they unloaded inside with her.

I happily sent him off to eat the cum overflowing out of his wife. But he was intercepted by my two friends to clean them up. When he finished with them, he walked over to his wife and resumed to clean her up again. While he did that I slathered on some lube and took a crack at the asshole for old time's sake. He was probably more eager about getting fucked than she was, throwing his ass back me at great speed like it was our last fuck as the world was coming to an end.

Covered in sweat and watching his new bride look on in disbelief, I shot my load deep inside his hold and told him to push it out so she could see it.

I knew after that day that neither one of them were bound to separate. In a way, I knew with their secrets out in the open about their love of dick should have bonded them forever. What I didn't expect as I was visiting a freaky-deaky shop was to find her face plastered on the cover box as some sweet-faced white girl taken advantage of by some big black men while her husband was in the gay section pretty much looking the same.

48 & 50

"You gonna let me melt in this bitch, aintcha boy," his voice whispered deep, raspy, and soulfully into my ear.

The perverse yet soothing rich combination of "bitch" and "boy" seemed to make me reluctantly weak and heatedly turned on all at the same time. He was my self-proclaimed top man, top daddy, therefore—as he so eloquently put it—I was conceived for the sole purpose of being his bottom boy.

As he dragged his big hefty dick down the tail end of my sweat-slick crack, making his hard muscled body comfortable on my back, there was absolutely no doubt in my mind that he was going to do everything in his almighty power to make me "sing" real pretty for him. And if I wasn't before that night, he was destined to make me his bitch-in-waiting by morning.

I was nervous, of course, and scared and a bit jumpy. Because, with a foolishly drunken flare, I had presented a woefully-skilled master with an unwrapped virgin rump roast eager to be plucked and pillage for his convenience. For reasons unknown, I thought *this* man to be most deserving of this gift. He was, in the truth, the essence of a real man, a man like me, or one that I woke up each morning striving to be, one that I desperately woke up needing to be.

As that big daddy dick raked itself down my lower part of my spine into the top of my virgin crack, sliding over my puckered hairy hole, I was hooked to the incredible sensation I denied myself for way too long. I had become everything I had told myself I was not. I could not be or ever fathom, with spine tingling sensations accompanied by violent body tremors of ecstasy and an eerie sense of calm.

Shit, I was horny and ready.

My urgent need for him to be in me must have had to supersede his want to be in of me. And after so many years of following my cream-stuffed dick into the deep trenches, I finally understood the eagerness and the willing surrender of every bottom I had ever fucked in my life.

Yet, in my euphoric state of mind, my real intellect came back into my senses, reminding me that in order for this to work, I needed to be worked open, as I replaced the countless cries in my ears have endured over the years.

Ouch, it hurts!
It won't fucking go in!
Ow, take it out of me!
Noooo!
Please! It feels like I'm being divided into twenty-two!

I could take the time to rewrite history, telling myself that I was honestly a truly noble man and gave into every one of those blubbering requests with the hopes that he would give into mine. But I didn't—often believing that I was put on this wide green earth for the comforts of my own aggressive needs. Sometimes, if it was more than just another piece of anonymous ass, I would treat it to a finger-fuck or a tongue-bath. If it wasn't, oh well, they were just guilty of being in the company of a fucking jackass with a ridiculously big dick, ramming my piece of hard steel up any exposed piece of ass crack with no mercy or wanton concern for anything other than myself.

Please, please, oh fucking please! Don't let me just another piece of ass! I reasoned with him strongly in my head.

It was too late.

I felt the worthless son of a bitch behind me, balancing his study body on one had while taking the other and guiding the budding head of that big bad prick over my wrinkled poop chute.

Please, I ain't asking for much, you worthless fuck. Just something, anything that will make taking you inside of me a teensy weensy bit easier.

My body jumped from the searing pain, feeling what felt like every fucking millimeter burrowing down into my tight sphincter.

Oh, no! Oh, fuck! Fuck you, man! Damn! No!

The pain was too excruciation, and my helpless body went completely rigid with my pulsating erection pinned down between my cramping legs, offering up the muffled screams my mouth just couldn't seem to get out of the mattress.

"Relax, shit," he said cowardly, making me tense up more that I thought I could. "I know you gave some lame chump some of this good *tight* ass before."

Somehow telling this chump the truth now would sound like some sort of bad come on line, like an invitation, so I said nothing. Giving it everything in my power to try to relax and give in to him.

As I quickly found out, patience wasn't a virtue of his.

Instead, like an agitated lowbred, he pushed in with full unrelenting force, not giving two shits that there was an actual human being attached at the end of his pulsing battering ram.

I wanted to cuss, but everything in my heart just stopped short of it.

Damn. For one, I knew if he was anything like me in his position he would be turned on, intoxicated by the power, and would level everything he had into me from here to now one, fine tuning the screams he could muster out of me. Secondly, I was quickly reminded of my countless victims, those that may or may not have enjoyed this.

"Ain't use to having a man on this broad back of yours, I see." He whispered hot in my ear, with an evil laced in his tone. "I'll be more than happy to change for you. It's a *long time* since the last time I broke in a fine saddle."

I wanted to shake him off just then, off my back, out my mind, but the more he worked his way inside of me the less I wanted to resist all the pangs and angst of this all.

It had been a long time coming—I deserved the consequences of this.

I tried to relax, a little more than just giving in, feeling the waves of cool air starting to build up, and riding through the airing crack of my bubble butt.

"Look at this damn jimmie, stretching and plunging that sweet bad ass. Ha!"

Then, like a psychotic break, my voice betrayed me, scornfully and soulfully in a murmur, "Get that ass!"

A hard slap came across my ass followed by the words, "Wake up, Sleeping Booty."

I awoke, stirring from my lay on my hard naked stomach.

Damn! It was all a dream.

A simple yet complicated fantasy that was on the verge of coming true before this bastard pulled me away from that bastard.

His face often changed with the frequency of the seasons, yet he always remained the same in my dreams: tall, black, superb, and muscle-bound like a real macho man should be. His hue transcended across the earthen rainbow from the blackest of blue to the pastiest of pale albinos, the chocolate-dipped G.I. Joe to the burly caramel-colored football player ready to tackle to having a biscuit-brown physique with muscles on top of bulging muscles.

He was ultimately a mature-looking reflection of me.

Masculine. Man.

"Wake up, Sleeping Booty," crooned Calvin, my tall and dark roommate delivering another cold hard slap against my bare ass.

"That's a motherfucking shame!" His friend Willie added, with his cute golden face but short malnourished body.

"All that sculpted perfection, and he ain't giving it up to a soul."

"He better gets his ass up and get to work before gets his ass handed to him."

"I'm just saying," Willie continued. "A brotha got needs, man!"

I felt his cold hand hovering over my warm ass.

"Don't you dare motherfucker," I grumbled, rolling out of bed and sliding my size sixteen boats into my slippers.

"What?" Willie asked naively.

"I got dick, too." I said shuffling my way to the bathroom across the hall. "Why don't you offer to tend to it sometimes? Save me the trouble of getting up and taking a piss when all you had to do was open your mouth to wash the shit out."

"Damn, Willie," Calvin said. "Some motherfucker got up on the wrong side of the bed this morning."

"No," I barked with the door wide open, pulling my dick through the slit of my boxers, taking a leak and a fart right in the heart of toilet water. "I got up to the wrong man riding my dick."

"Aw, don't tell me my man is still salty that he has to act like a big boy?" Calvin mocked.

"Fuck you." I snapped, throwing up my middle finger.

"That's part of the reason we came in here." Willie snapped back.

"What? You gonna let me and Cal run a train on that high-yella ass? It's been a minute since I got into old-fashioned Chattanooga choo-choo!" I laughed stuffing my dick back into my boxers, coming back across the hall to the bedroom.

"Fuck you, man," Willie said testily.

"Nah, bitch, I'm trying to fuck your sweet ass." I said in the doorway, as my twelve-incher rushed with blood down my leg. "Case and fucking point."

"Nasty ass," Willie said disgusted.

I knew that look all too often. It was a bit of jealousy for being blessed with so much of a plantain for a dick tied in with a feverous lust and an urgent worry about what it could do to a person after it was all crammed into them, or at least that was always the goal.

But, being me, I responded with "only if that's what you got? There's a bathroom over there if you need to clean up—or out."

Calvin wanted to laugh, but being that Willie was his boy and he had secreted told me that Willie was raped repeatedly by this big dick tyrant in a halfway house, he didn't. Neither one of them said anything and just looked at me with their arms folded.

I had no response either.

I must admit though I was just a little salty at them for no real reason at all, other than for my own selfish faults. It was bad just waking up from a half-rested sleep. On top of that, waking up to the rigmarole of being harass from a dream that I finally getting into. But I was bitter, most of all, because at the tender age of thirty-five, I was for the first time in my life was an on-the-books employee.

Don't get me wrong, I always worked. My dick and my demeanor was my first trade with my close second being a jack of all trades. The problem was, while I was smart enough to save my money from all the money gifts that I received from the men and women that I messed around with along with always taking payment under the table, it pretty much left me without much of a paper trail. So while I got all these safe deposit boxes with all this money, with close to three-fourths of a million dollars in total, I can't do shit. I can't open a bank account because the way the bank saw it I never held down a job to justify the deposits, which could probably be seen as suspect. Most people worry about having enough credit or repairing bad credit. But because I never was indebted to anybody or needed anything from the system, I didn't have credit whatsoever. And without credit, to the world I simply did not exist.

Back when I was younger, it was like dirt off my shoulders to get some rich sugar mama (or cougar they call them now) or some dick-crazed fag to get me what I wanted. If I wanted a car, they would lease it. If I wanted a condo, not only would they sign for it they would take care of all expenses including healthcare and whatever else. And even on the off-chance I had to come out of pocket for anything, I knew how to buy it at auction or tap into the black market.

The funniest thing was that I wasn't slipping in any shape or form. I was what the old folks said "growing into my handsomeness." I was eating right and exercising, giving my body that true diesel cut that made many of the professional bodybuilders envious. In fact, if I wanted to upgrade my game that was the perfect time.

As I began dancing into my thirties, I decided I wanted something of my own. Something I could buy free and clear, in my own name and in my own right, without the hassle of being questioned about the source of my income.

Unfortunately, that wasn't as easy as it sounded. Even with my expertise and experience, in various fields, because I had a criminal record to my name, employers wasn't exactly clamoring over one another to offer me a job. But in order to do what I needed to do I had to get one that, even at a minimum, paid me legitimately.

I had nearly given up on my search when Calvin, my pre-opt transsexual girlfriend's gay play cousin (I don't make this shit up) slashed housemate shot me a line that the Bishop Brothers was looking for a third permanent muscle man in their family-owned repo and tow business.

Although I had done everything under the sun from being a shade tree mechanic to a bouncer to a bookkeeper to a cameraman, the business of repossessions never crossed my path. Then it became instantly obviously that it could have a totally legitimate side while offering an incredible itch that needed to be scratched with underworld possibilities.

I was fortunate enough to meet the Bishop Brothers "strict" requirements of being big, black, and intimidating just like them. Now when it came to working, I was never against the work, regardless of what I was doing. I may was against giving Uncle Sam his share of the cut, in the past, but *hard work* was definitely a word that was a good friend of mine. And boy, it should go without saying that work put a hurting on me in those first two weeks, putting in some fourteen hours plus of hard labor each day for minimum pay. Not to be confused with minimum wage, but given all that I was doing plus time and a half I should've been paid a hell of a lot more. It was so much so physically draining that I spent every weekend sound asleep in bed, mildly reluctant to get up to go to work the following Monday.

"There you go, you look nice, son," Willie complimented me on my standard-issued gray uniformed jumper. He thought by giving me an encouraging word from time to time would keep me motivated.

I had to tell myself that while I thought he was trying to be funny, he was well intentioned, especially by the way Willie felt up on my diesel cut pecs as I fought hard the urge to hang his sweet ass out of the second story window just for kicks.

It was five o'clock in the fucking morning and I was once again overwhelmed by sleep to say anything back or slap the shit out of him, so I just looked at him and flashed him a sardonic smile.

The Bishop Brothers had their rinky-dink little set up in the rough part of town. It wasn't much, rent was extremely cheap, and it was never really suppose to have been anything other than a place for them to keep their paperwork. My job was to report there first to get my hands on the fully comprehensive list of all the assignments that needed to be taken care of that day. This was regardless of the fact that most likely there were still dozens of jobs left over from the day before or the day before that that needed to be tended to as well.

I hated it all, the work but most specifically the neighborhood. It wasn't like it was the safest place to be period, but that time of morning wasn't all that grand either. By the time I had to report to work, it was too late for the riff-rafts to do any harm without running the risk that the police might've came on their shift ready to change the world, and it was too early for the decent folks to make their appearances to complain. It didn't help either that the place sat right on the dividing line of gang territory. And it wasn't so much about the reporting to office that I had the beef with as much as it was the time I spent in the morning waiting on someone to open up the damn building, so that I could get in. Leaving me out in the cold to look out at the neighborhood of doom and gloom, with no hope or prospect whatsoever of a better day with it surrounded by short rundown high-rises and dilapidated warehouses.

It was the job of their secretary Maggie to be there early enough to bring in from the cold, but it was usually Leroy, one of the owners, coming in from his overnight shift that beat her to the punch.

He would just look at me every morning standing there cold, shake his head, pull out his key and let me in.

Leroy was the elder of the two partnering brothers. He was a big man at six-foot-six, creeping shy of a lean three hundred pounds. He did something in the military way back when, and his body still thanked him for it handsomely at fifty. He could even still take off his shirt and wow most people half his age, showing off an impeccable six-pack and a nice broad chest with those old-fashioned arms that were molded out of hard manual labor. Not by working out at some prissy gym, though I would've been too surprised that he did that, too. His face however was a different story. The best way I could describe it was that he looked like he lived a hard life. Either that life lived him hard. He wasn't much to look at in the face with his barely-there low crop cut of salt-and-pepper hair, which made him look about a good ten years older than he really was. He had one of those old-school Army sergeant rough-hard faces, equipped with the signature wisp of a haired upper lip with the exaggerated frown lines that ran from the bottom of his irritated bloodshot eyes to the top of his defined rounded chin. It was the kind of face that was waiting on you to screw up just so he could get the opportunity to jack you up.

Leroy always came off to be as being the more responsible of the two brothers. Being that when he worked he worked. He worked like a dog. Like his life depended on it. The downside to that or to Leroy rather was that even though he was in business, owned a business, he was a far cry from being a businessman. At least, being a savvy one, at that. Because anybody with two eyes could see that his business should have been much more profitable than he complained it was. And it wasn't like he was so much of a control freak as he was paranoid. He was so worried about getting screwed over that he failed to listen to any kind of reason, not even from his partners, which consisted of a third brother that I never laid eyes on.

Joe, the younger brother by two years and the other partner, usually came in about a good five minutes after we did. No matter when we came in, early or late, it was always five minutes later. Right down to the very second. Because it always felt like he was watching us from afar somewhere counting. That was how uncanny timing was. I remember that so well because he usually came in after I warmed up just enough to brew up a pot of coffee. Unlike Leroy, Joe was quite handsome, and stood taller at six-eight. If I was to say that Leroy was a soft milk chocolate brown, I would have to say that Joe was more of a sensual chocolate color with a splash of cream. He sort of put me into mind of a younger version of a man I knew long ago, from a sexual escapade near the crown of a bathhouse rooftop, except next to his brother his bulk didn't look quite as refined. Yet he was still in great shape, very well put together with his hard round muscled belly, but his frame looked more ballooned altogether; more puffed up like a bone crusher than anything else.

In a former life, Joe was a crooked cop with a second career as a sex-crazed womanizer. In spite of having a fox of a wife waiting on him at home, Joe loved talking about his many lines of pussy. It was funny listening to him to him talk about it, because he did so with the same fanaticism of that of a teenage boy about to get some for the very first time. It was even funnier the way his crotch bulged in those jumpers as he talked, and tried hard not to grab his one-eyed brother. But the thing I like most about Joe was his ass. He had one of the most incredible asses I had ever seen. It was full and plump and muscled and stuffed tight in his jumpers, and I wanted to do everything in my power to set it free, so that I could eat it, lick it, and stick it to my heart's content. I remembered thinking that if I really ever got into fucking some old ass (not like just going in for a nutt but somebody I could kick it with) that his ass would be the kind of ass I wanted presented to me. Young or old, it really didn't matter, but it seemed like the older some men get the fuller their asses get too, like tree rings or something.

And then, about a good twenty to thirty minutes later, Maggie, their secretary, would come in.

She came in apologizing for being so late again, for one reason or another, and Leroy would get at her about it. He was stern but never serious with her, as it became apparent it was very much a part of their routine. She would sometimes break the usual humdrum, after rushing to get the computer on to give me what I needed, by complaining to me about her husband, her two kids, and the drama that unfolded the night before with one family member or another.

For a woman with such a traditional name, she had a ground-breaking beauty that sort of got lost in her ditzy demeanor. As I stood out in the cold sometimes, I could have been a thousand times more sympathetic if I felt she genuinely feared being harassed in such a dreadful neighborhood. I wouldn't do that to any woman, in particular a pretty one like that. But she was late for being late, and that was all there was to it. She knew full well that she had job security on several fronts: She was the brothers' niece through marriage by way of that other brother, and the only one they truly trusted to handle their paperwork. But her ace in the hole—the way it was told to me—was that she had brothers and other blood relatives on both sides of the proverbial gangland fence to ward off theft and tagging and any gang wars nearby, seeing that both sides had a common interest in her.

So between her and Joe, I got an earful every morning with my cup of coffee and donut. Leroy was only so fortunate to hide in the back, where the kitchen was, waiting on the Verdict to come out. The Verdict was my job, or rather a list of jobs that I needed to do that day, which heavily hinged on Leroy parting with some of his hard-earned money for the day.

While their business was mainly repossessions, the Bishop Brothers got into everything under the sun and had a vehicle for every occasion. They had tow trucks for both cars and commercial-grade trucks. They had a straight-lined truck for moving, and a dump truck with a lift to haul junk. They even had a couple of junk vehicles, including an old passenger bus that they never got around to using. And there was rumored to have been a big rig sleeper truck off-site somewhere. This ironically worked heavily in both of our favors. In a previous life, when I was dying of boredom as a kept gigolo, I came up with this weird personal challenge of obtaining a license in every class of driving. I could drive anything from a motorcycle to a paratransit bus to a tanker with placards.

Leroy and I both preferred towing, which was pretty much what he did in the overnight hours. Unfortunately, the daytime hours didn't afford that kind of luxury being that most people most likely were out driving their soon-to-be repossessed vehicles. That was unless we had enough jobs to warrant such a deal. And even that was a bit iffy depending on certain factors or whatever was more pressing coming down the pipe.

At any rate, the difference between towing and everything else was that if I had to do anything else, it pretty much meant that I would have to hire somebody else to help me out.

Leroy hated giving me money for a crew, which could easily run a few hundred dollars each day plus any additional fees and expenses.

So after Maggie printed Joe and I out our list, we tallied the number of jobs that we had to do. It could range from towing to outside contract repossessions to eviction removal to foreclosure removal to hauling junk. Again, it was whatever came down that pipe. This worked out well in my favor because Joe like to get down and dirt with the hard stuff, and was such a cheap bastard that he tried to bypass paying for a crew by taking on everything himself. (Plus, I figured when he got dirty like that it gave him a reasonable excuse to drop in on one of his women.) Once we got that settled, who was going to do what, I mapped out my route for the day and handed Leroy the verdict.

We were usually happy with the results at first, because it meant that Leroy got his way and I got mine. But, then, somebody always threw a wrench in our beautiful plans. I mean, always. Since it was a family business, there was always somebody that wanted to come in for the day to earn some extra money. And it always seemed to be with somebody that

Joe couldn't work with because of some kind of prior falling out with. This often meant that my plans had to change so that they didn't have to deal with one another and that family member or friend could still break bread.

The worst of these offenders was Mac, Leroy's beastie boy of a son, who was always trying to score a quick payday.

Take everything I said to describe Leroy, minus his moustache, make him about twenty-five years younger, age him about fifteen years to look about forty-something, miniaturize him to about six-one and there he was.

The hilarity behind Mack was that he and Joe *actually* got along. The problem was that they got along too well. Unlike his father Leroy who was all about work, Mack was all about getting some pussy much like his uncle. He was always on the hunt for it, and was never shy about expressing his insatiable hunger for it. Scrapping up his earning to hire more prostitutes or to buy liquor to share with his lady friends to get them drunk enough to get them to bed. In short, it meant that Joe and Mack couldn't work together because very little work would have ever gotten done.

Naturally, I liked Mack. We were close to the same age, and had more in common with each other than with anybody else there. He wasn't much to look at during a conversation, but he had that sort of on-point personality that made a person forget about his tough mug. He forever talked a good game worth of shit while we worked. Even to the point he made some days bearable and others worth looking forward to again.

He never showed it but he sort of gave me the vibe that he got down. He was the type to quickly defend that he didn't get "punked." My suspicions were only confirmed one day after my he-she girlfriend Priscilla picked me up after worked and told me that Mack and his boys used to jump her back in the day. Sometimes treating her like a punching back, other times strengthening a bond of brotherhood by jamming her in succession. Their gang roughing her up soon became an aphrodisiac that led him to pimp her back in the day.

...

"Stroke that bitch back on this dick." I cajoled, holding my baby steady by the small of "her" back. Ever so often I had to give that phat Creole ass a hard smack and watch her wiggle it back against me, fighting hard to sink in every inch. "Stroke it back. Stroke it back, trick. There you go! Take this dick!"

I held on tighter to her sweaty skin, pumping harder and faster listening to her sing real pretty for me in a soulful melody of high squeals and low pants. I was melting even deeper into what was left of her pummeled walls, soaking further open to let me up in that, and trying hard to gobble it with the same bite as a tighter hole. I was her man. She was my good bitch. And I could tell that this bitch was as hot as a firecracker that I had brought her closer to the edge than I wanted to. So I knew that I had to up the ante before that hole showed me a thing or two, dead bolting around my dick.

I reached forward, cupped her by her neck with one hand slightly pulling her upright and grabbed her by the corner of her mouth with the other. I let her scream to the top of her mind. Letting the quiet house, the sleeping neighborhood getting an earful of what she was going through on the awful end of my twelve-inch poker that she loved so much.

"C'mon, pussy bitch, don't act like you're a stranger to this dick now!" I said calmly pounding at her twitching hole for everything it was worth.

I listened to her do her and my low-hanging family jewels do them, sounding a relentless drumbeat that made for a sweet background noise against her foreground noise.

"That's it, trick. There you go!"

I was riding that shit hard.

I was ready to either break that back in or blow that back out. So much so that it almost afforded me the luxury of almost driving in balls deep. Of course, she fought back. It was already hard enough for her to recover from the amount of dick she had in her makeshift womb. But as her man, I had to let her know that I was in control of this shit. When I got that she got it through her hardheaded skull, I threw her face back into the mattress before reaching forward to grab a sizeable chunk of her black and blond weave.

She screamed as I roughly pulled it back. Ever so often letting my vice grip go just enough so she could relax her neck—but just enough. I pulled and pulled harder and let go just enough to pull it again, sometimes harder than I should've just get the adrenaline another boost.

"Oh, Gawd!" She whimpered with her large tits knocking loudly together to her own little stump of a joint slinging back to tickle my nutt sac.

I did her like this for a long while.

She was letting me know how much of a bitch in heat she was and how much she loved this big ole man-dick digging out her stretched guts.

Priscilla got her fix, that was a given, and it would have been enough for me too if I wasn't always aiming to be an overachiever in bed.

I was more than a big dick. I knew how to work it.

I spun her onto her back, pounding her hard once again with my large hand around her delicate neck. She loved it this way the most. She loved looking that the disgust and the brute of man fucking her, nearly choking the life out of her pretty womanly body. Her hole got wetter, slicker. Her face almost flushed, and that hormone-shrunken dick of hers just oozing a puddle of pre-cum onto her stomach. She was almost to the point of blacking out. I clasped her dick and gave it a solid tug. My touch delivered her from her milk that splattered across her belly.

It was too much.

"Oh, got damn!" I rowdily growled. "Oh, shit!"

I let go of her neck, and pumped away to my content, only to watch her come to just in time to shudder from the white-hot load that blasted its way through her intestines.

"Ah, yeah," I exhaled. "That's what I'm talking about. Whoo!"

I caught my breath, and let the pressure of what I let go ease me out of her flooded hole before collapsing on the bed next to the winded she-male.

I let her get her bearings before instructing her to get out there and fix me a club sandwich with those veggie sticks chips she got me hooked on. That order also wordlessly included a screwdriver (vodka and orange juice) to go with my breakfast.

Hey, it wasn't a traditional breakfast, but it was what I needed to keep up my stamina up for the day.

Work was hard, but home was even harder with all of its intricacies and stuff. We lived in a nice two-story house on a small lot in the rundown section of town. It wasn't too bad of a place like it was where I worked. There was a strong sense of safety but it didn't always come with a strong sense of security, if that made any sense. The neighborhood was old enough to find comfort in stability. Yet, because so many of the younger generations were taking off where their parents left off, there wasn't much in appreciating what they had, at least with some of them. Our street had its lonely drug house a few houses up the way and we occasionally heard a gunshot or two blaring in the nearby distance. But it was no big deal. Not to us. We figured it was what it was, or I did. The thing that constantly worked my nerve was that the other neighbors often feel in and out of favor with each other every few days, and constantly wanted to update the neighborhood of the status of their friendships. Even in the late night hours. One day they would be outside laughing and joking and playing their music extremely loud. The next day or so later they were out in the street cussing each other out and divulging all of their business, only to repeat the cycle again a day or two later.

If that wasn't enough, I had to contend with the stuff that went on within our house with Priscilla, her play cousin Calvin, and the many rest of them.

The best way I could describe my relationship with Priscilla was that we were sort of like fuck buddies with marital benefits. Of course, I was her husband, and she wanted to be my wife. The tragedy was that I wasn't all that serious about us like that. The way she wanted to be. Then, I was at a place in my life where good food and good sex and the ability to keep a stable roof over my head were good enough. I was no longer trapped in the belief that I was destined to commit my dick to just one hole for any serious amount of time. Priscilla was like most girls and gay boys in their early twenties: She was going to show me how good it was to have her as a girlfriend, as a possible wife, by catering to my every need whenever I needed. But until I saw "the light" she was content with having me in her bed every night. And I saw no harm in treating her like a wifey.

The difference between the roles of a wife *and a* wifey *is that a wife gets all the proper respect of one, with or without the paperwork. Whereas the wifey has first dibs on the dick but isn't the only chick in the line up.*

That didn't mean Priscilla held her breath out on me. Even though she was young, she had been around the block a few times to know the game. She knew that although it would have been nice if I stuck around and settled down, men like me usually didn't. We had our fun and eventually moved on. Moreover, even though having a man was a priority, her top priority was going through with her sex change operation. And for that, she needed money. As awful as it may sound, since I wasn't invested in having a relationship with her, I was even less invested in her to even offer to help pay for it with some of the stashed away money I had elsewhere. She was a smart enough girl not to ask, knowing that I was too well put together to be as broke as I claimed I was. So she tricked on the sly, as an orphan this time, when she thought I wasn't around. I guess she thought it was better than the alternative, of this sugar daddy that was willing to pay for the transition outright along with whatever else that was needed. The catch was that she would be stuck to him. He was a good guy, from what I heard, had money to circle a few lifetimes. But I think she was repulsed at the idea of being stuck to a wealthy man that was just as big of a queen as she was.

I wasn't crying over spilled milk with her extracurricular activities. Like I said, I didn't really care. She was young and destined to do young and foolish things. Besides, I was getting my extra paper, too. Old habits die hard. I was boning these two older broads from around the way along with getting with this drug dealer that had a mad hankering for sucking dick. He was willing to blow through his fat knot (money) to get a taste of mine. Which, of course, was when I wasn't too tired from work and shit to do anything with them. After I started my job though, seeing any of them became far and few between.

Then, of course, there was Calvin, my friend and fellow top, with his revolving door of boy toys from down in the basement, and Willie, with his skinny ass, tried to keep up with whatever he could get a hold of anywhere. The other roommates, Aron and Tyrone, pretty much kept to themselves on the main floor and were hardly ever home.

Last but certainly not least was Cynthia, a drag queen that Priscilla referred to as her "gay" mother, who dominated the basement with her lair of misfits and runaways. They were all young and queer and starting around the age of sixteen. Most however were like eighteen and nineteen and up, struggling to find their footing in the world and in the gay life. Since so many of them broke, being minimum wage earners or college students or both, and I usually needed to build a crew, I thought I would be help in hiring from the pick of the limp wrist litter.

Most of them weren't interested in the money as much as it was about them hanging out with me, by chance, the star of their show.

It gave the queerest of them a ray of hope that if "Ms." Priscilla could land a man like me, it was hope for the rest of them, too. Being so young and impatient, it didn't leave much chance for them to go out and eventually find that special man on their own. They wanted me and weren't ashamed to tell it to my face. I would be lying if I said those Rolodexes of innocent crushes didn't stroke the ego just a bit. But some were just full-fledged obsessions that were even scary for a big man like me.

In any case, those weren't too squeamish about manual labor would jump to the front of the line to spend the entire day with me. They would work enough get my attention and then pose, trying hard not to sweat a drop in their attempt to still look as cute as they thought they did. It was comical at first before I realized that I could've done a whole lot more on my own.

I had no interest in any of them. Not even the cute ones.

In my book, all of them were too young, even though the majority of them were of legal tender. Aside from the blatantly obvious, I knew I was packing too much dick for them to be playing with that early in the game regardless of the fact that their freshly-driven hormones were telling them otherwise. Now that I was wise enough to know better and wasn't solely driven by lust anymore, I knew that my dick was too large of a rarity to ruin some naïve young buck like that. For it to be an enjoyable experience for then, I mean. There were scores of other men that were destined to come along. And given that those biology books often said that I was twice the average size, I said to myself that it was only right that they have as much fun with those first and then come get at me in about five or ten years.

But that didn't mean I gave up on hiring the boarders from the house. I was just more selective in the process. The only ones that really put their backs into their work were the young masculine studs that were providing sexual favors to whomever to keep a roof over their head. Still young enough to feel like sex was "nothing but a thing," just good steady practice for later on down the road. Yet, I knew from experience that after awhile that could grow tiresome enough to feel like a chore. Especially when there was a dependency factor involved and the other person knew how to take full advantage of it. Even in spite of that, I also knew that living in a houseful of eccentric sissies henpecking about a whole bunch of nonsense could drive the sanest of macho men up the wall. So, for most of the hunks-in-training that were afraid that their ways were going to rub off of them, they had a deep itch for something that was going to tap into their cavemen instincts, needing to prove their self-worth through "manly" things of the non-sexual nature.

And then there was Willie.

■■■

"It's about fucking time," Willie said, slamming the door of the company's box truck with the excitement of a kid on Christmas morning written across his face.

Willie was one of those ex-cons that were fortunate enough to find employment shortly after being released from prison. His main job was part-time as a day laborer, with very short hours and very early in the morning detailing cars before auctions. Meanwhile, the rest of the time or the rest of the day rather, whenever I needed an extra man on my crew, I knew that I could always count on Willie to come through.

Willie was a damn good worker, very determined. He had that sort of old-school mentality to work. He believed wholeheartedly in making his hard-earned money whenever he could and of course had a strong work ethic to boot. I didn't always call on him, though. Unlike some of the other folks in the house that were penniless, he did have somewhat of a stable income coming in. I really tried hard to give everyone a chance to earn a little something-something. Some took graciously. Others, for whatever reason, were allergic to the work, holding their breaths on someone to whisk in and offer them a high-paying job with no skills and full benefits.

Willie was always there ready with a smile. He just needed to know when I was coming through to pick him up. His handsome smile seemed to increase threefold after I put the money in his hand after a job or two or a full day's work, and happily reminded me that if I needed him again I knew where to find him.

Willie was about a good ten years younger than me, and going through with what I was going through to get into the system, I told him that if he was serious about being counted that I could put in a good word for him with the Bishop Brothers. It would not only mean more money for him, but in the same breath it spared the brothers from coming out of pocket so much with hiring and negotiating with different people all the time. Nevertheless, Willie was still young and in love with idea of keeping a hundred percent on the dollar, blind to the cost. He was just like me, thought he had plenty of time before he became an "old man" get put in. I wasn't old, but dammit did time fly. As much as I wanted to, I couldn't get mad at him for following my mistakes. I warned him at least. That was all I could do. It was more than anybody did for me.

On that particular day I picked up Willie from the house, I also had one of the young new studs from the basement with me in truck. We went about the business of going place to place, setting stuff out of apartments and houses, picking over what we could, and doing it again. Before for long, ten hours had passed and we got most things on the list done and I was ready to call it an early day. Usually being the good guy that I am, I would treat my crew (those that stayed with me most of the day) to dinner at some sit-down buffet-style restaurant, taking the liberty of paying them after I paid the check.

I didn't even get a chance to do that before the kid, the third wheel our crew, got his food and took of into the sunset without cause, concern, or with his hard-earned money. I tried to call him back to at least give him that, knowing that it wasn't above most drug addicts and some other head cases to see the tangibles immediately in front of them and walk off. It wasn't common, but it wasn't that uncommon either. Going from something quite laughable in the beginning to something quite sad overtime.

Since Willie was the only one that I had to worry about getting back home now, I decided to take him back to the office with me. I wasn't about to drive all the way across town just to drop him off at home and then come back to drop off the truck just to go back home. I didn't think too much of it, and because it was something that I did a few times out of the week I knew it wasn't that big of a deal. But as soon as I stepped into the office with Willie by my side, I instantly felt this tension that oozed between him, Joe and Mack, who were standing around the coffee pot flapping their gums, more than likely talking about their favorite subject P-U-S-S-Y.

I didn't know what to make of it at first, the tension. So I treaded lightly, stepping around whatever it was between the three of them like it was a minefield. I excused myself to make a quick run upstairs to where Leroy kept a makeshift apartment. Leroy was still somewhat paranoid about me. Not because of my record, but because I was still relatively new and I wasn't any sort of kin to him. And I was working harder than ever to win his trust by delivering any extra money he gave me earlier in the day back.

It wasn't that I was all that greatly honest. In a younger life, I would've gladly kept every dime, making up some bogus excuse for needing to spend every penny. For me, though, it wasn't even about the money. Like I said before, I was good on that end. I just knew that in order for me to have more peace at the job, while I was there, I needed him to give me some leeway in the trust department. It was already a hard job, and I knew from personal experience that it was only going to get a bit easier once he gave in about an inch. The first inch is always the hardest.

I got to the top of the stairs, and just before I got ready to knock on the door, I heard the cot in his room squeak. It wasn't like one or two squeaks like somebody was on or in the bed. It was a lot more to it. Yet, it wasn't enough for me to suspect that there was someone else in there with him. Leroy was a lot of things, but he wasn't a cheat like his brother. He knew where his bread was buttered with his wife of thirty-some-odd years, which I think was the reason he worked so hard. It was one thing to provide. It was whole other season to run himself ragged like he did. He didn't have much going on in the face. Meaning, he wasn't much to look at. In his defense, I was quite sure that he made his wife very happy every time he took of his shirt and showed off his mature chiseled frame that made even my mouth water. And I couldn't see it hurting that he remained gainful employed throughout their years of matrimony.

The bed squeaked louder and louder, and then stopped. Leroy took a deep sigh of relief. The way it sounded through the door I knew that he wasn't having sex with anybody else, mainly because of the video still playing in the background with the people shouting to orgasm in the background. I waited for a minute, slowly treading softly down the stairs and quickly running hard up them, knocking on the door.

"Who is it?" Leroy asked in his hoarse drill sergeant voice.

"Me." I said calmly.

"Hold on a minute."

I did. He came to the door a second later with his shirt off in his boxer brief sporting a fine-looking basket accompanied by the whiff a musty dick.

"What you need, son?" He said less agitated than usual.

"I came up give you this." I said, showing him seven twenty dollar bills in a nice crisp fold.

He grunted, took it, and closed the door.

I made my way back down the stairs not knowing what to except to find when I got down there. It seemed that everybody was exactly where I left them, but not like in a good way. It was almost as if Joe and Mack were waiting on Willie to make one false move before he gave them permission to attack. Not all that concern about it anyway since it didn't really have anything to do with me, I escorted Willie out of the building and into my truck.

As we safely retreated home, Willie kept on asking me did I work with them. He kept on asking and asking as if my answer was suddenly going to change, as if his eyes were deceiving him that he couldn't see for himself that we all had on the same uniform. I tried to get inside of his head, to see where it was or was going, but he kept shutting me out. He didn't want to talk about it.

The next day I showed up at work to find that the building already opened. This was a huge surprise given that every morning since I began working there I had to spend the greater part of my morning standing in front of it instead of in it—even days I thought I was showing up later so I didn't have to. I was flabbergasted when I found Joe there alone brewing up a pot of coffee.

"Hey, what's goin' on brothaman?" He asked in his engine-rattling voice, pouring coffee in mug.

"Nothing much," I said. "What got you here this early in the mornin'?"

"I work here." He said in a teasing tone.

"For real," I giggled at his humorous expression.

"Early morning with one of my bitches," he smiled handing my cup off. "We got goin' about an hour ago, and it was a split between goin' to sleep and coming in late listening to my blood whine about me being more responsible. Like those two years he got over me make that much of a freakin' difference! You know how it goes?"

"Nah," I grinned. "I'm usually out in front waiting on him."

"Nah, nah," he shook his head stuffing his mouth with a breakfast sandwich. "I ain't talkin' about Leroy. I'm talkin' about that good pussy that put a brothaman to sleep after getting that nutt-nutt. You know what I'm sayin'?"

"Oh, oh, yeah, no doubt," I said. "You got to be more clearer when you speak with your mouth full like that."

"That's what she said." He laughed.

"What?" I said, missing what he said.

"It's from some corny-ass show I was watchin' last night. It'll take forever for that bitch to explain."

"Okay," I agreed.

"If you knew the joke you would understand," he said still rolling with laughter about it.

"Okay," I reiterated.

I took a sip from my mug and reached for a newly-bought package of store-bought donuts. I thought about what I could have said to make him erupt with laughter with his response. I got the joke then. I just chalked it up to being too early in the morning to be doing that kind of perverse thinking, so I didn't let on.

"That white boy was right. That shit works. I got to try it with better lines so it'll work better." He said more to himself than to me with his laughter quickly fading away.

If this was him opening up the building, I thought. *Then the cold wasn't all that bad.* He wouldn't have been such a pain if he hadn't been there so early, so different than usual. And because we were the only two there it wasn't like I could make a break elsewhere without it coming off as being ugly. Joe had enough people on his bad list with family and friends and I didn't wanted to be added to that massive club being that without Leroy it was just me and him.

After he got his laugh in, all that remained was a smile and he kept it on me. It wasn't the kind of smile that didn't just happen. It had some serious thought behind it, and about a thousand wheels were churning in his head.

"Spill it." I said with the anxiety was getting next to me.

"I noticed that you don't talk about pussy like we do. Ain't getting none? Or is that knobber you brought around here yesterday giving you all that you handle?"

"Huh? Oh, hell naw," I said in disgust. It was all part of an act, the down low act, and if I do say so myself a very good one. Look, it wasn't like I wasn't proud of the same-gender loving man that I was. I just knew *where* I was. It wasn't like I could say to him or anyone else that asked me in that neighborhood to accept me and get over it. No. Oh, hell no. And I wasn't so much worry about my job or staying in the system as much as I was worried about word getting around. It wasn't the people inside that I was worried about either. It was people on the outside. Men got killed just by looking at someone the wrong way. We were in the heart of gang territory, and if word got around that I was still a "pile driver" out of prison system, neither gang would hesitate to cut off my dick and feed it to me like they did in *Dead Presidents*. "He's just a roommate that needed to make some extra dough? What do you think is going on?"

"Your boy didn't say anything?"

"Nope," I said truthfully. "You know anything?""

"Hey, I don't know much. I just heard that your boy got a little sugar in his tank. I don't know if you caught what was going on yesterday, but apparently my nephew had to get you're boy straighten out a few years back for trying to look at his dick."

My instinct was to laugh, but I thought it could be dangerous since he might not have known that his beloved nephew was a booty bandit as well.

I played it cool. "I don't know nothing about that. He knows I worked here, and knew that we put a crew together to work from time to time. He was just with me to earn some dough, and since we were closer this way I didn't think much of it."

"Cool," he agreed. "Just watch your back around punks like that."

"No need," I laughed. "Most of those kinds of clowns like their shit packed in."

He laughed, breaking some of the building tension in the room.

"I remember that from my time in 'college.'" I said hiding behind code.

I told Leroy about my checkered past, but I wasn't sure if he told he told his brother.

"I'm glad you said something," Joe said seriously. "I know about you. That's part of the reason why I came in early to see you. My son, see, got into some trouble way back. The lawyer said that it ain't no way he goin' to get off easy, and I was wonderin' if there was something he could do so he didn't get took...punked?"

Unfortunately, it was the most secretive question that most people asked me when they or somebody they knew were about to head to the penitentiary. It was also the question that made me swell with guilty because I was one of the fortunate handfuls of convicts that was spared the tradition of inmate "initiation". It was something I was relieved about personally, but at the same time, it was something that I couldn't tell anybody. For one, most ex-cons weren't that lucky to tell my story. And two, most civilians might interpret it as a cover-up for something that happened. And being that I wasn't above climbing on a few backs to do some imitation of my own, it started to weigh on my conscious—just a bit (but we were in prison)—the friends and family that genuinely worried about guys like me.

"Well, I'm not going to lie. It does happen more often than most people would like to think. But it doesn't happen as much as movies and television would like you to believe, either," I assured him through lying. "Most people think it is limited to the lames, the loners, the runs, and the young bucks getting the short end of the stick. The truth is that most prisoners are mostly likely gunning to flip them through calculated means. Make them their bitch. So it won't go down unless he wants it too. That goes for folks that are too big or too small, too. They maybe an obvious target but they can ward off advances before it gets too deep.

"The thing is if he goes in there thinking for a second that he will be hemmed up, he already lost the battle because somebody is going to sniff it out and make his nightmares come true. That is if he's not gang related. I was spared the fire because I once ran with a petty street gang from back in the day that became affiliated with a national gang."

"So you're a gang banger?" Joe asked with raised eyebrows.

"Behind bars, by association," I said, "considering that me and my old childhood crew were still relatively tight and I hadn't switched over or betrayed them. As for participating in anything like the stuff that goes on out here, never that. We used to do some regular around-the-way shit like snatch purses and swipe stuff from the local convenient store, but nothing like the wild shit these kats out here are doing."

Joe took in my words. He wanted to say something else, but Maggie came in through the door, and mouthed that "we'll talk about it later." As soon as he disappeared, Leroy came in and told me to follow him upstairs. He never did that, and my stomach was constantly dropping thinking that I had done something wrong.

"You know why I called you up here?" Leroy asked with his back turned to me fumbling with something near the window.

"No, sir," I said.

"Yesterday, I sent you out to work and you came back with most of your shit done." He said turning around,

"Okay," I said, thinking all the while that that was my job but not knowing what else to say.

"I sent my numbskull of a brother out and he got nothing done." He paused.

I finally asked, "You sure that you meant to call me up here, sir?"

"Sure I'm sure."

"I'm not following, sir. Did you need my help with something?"

"Exactly," he smiled. "I knew you were a bright kid. I called you up here because I need you to do with Joe what you do with Mack. I need your help in coming up with a way to do without it coming off that he needs a babysitter."

"Sir, with all do respect, your brother is a grown-ass man. I don't think he's going to take too kindly to some stranger holding his hand—even on the sly."

"That's why it got to look like you ain't," he said, pulling out a thick wad of money. "I'm willing to pay you for your time."

"But, sir," I defended. "It ain't about the money."

"I know. This is everything you've ever given me back from the time that you've started working here. Why did you do it?"

"Honestly, to be honest, sir," I said. "I mean I know too many people aren't running to give men like me a chance to because I got record, thinking that I'm still my past. I figured what a better way show my appreciation for this job other than by doing my job the best I can and doing right by you and your business."

"You know what's called?"

"Yeah, integrity," I said.

"My point exactly," he said coming in closer, with his smile somehow smoothing out the hard edges of his face. "You may not have always had it or may have lost it along the way, but you as an ex-con got it back. My brother went to police academy and stayed on the police force for about twenty-five years, retired, and never knew what it was. He started out crooked and left crooked."

"If that's the case, it isn't much I can do about that."

"I know. But you can kind of keep him focus like you do my son."

"Sir," I laughed. "Mack and I are sort of peers. I'm older than him so he looks up to me. I don't think Joe is going to do the same with me. You know?"

Leroy looked at me sort of disappointed. It was obvious to him that I didn't want to do it. It was hard on me to get Mack to stay focus, I wasn't about to do it again with another one of his family members. "I understand."

"Maybe it'll get better once he finishes his thing with his son."

"His son?" Leroy asked surprised, thinking that he might have been taken aback that Joe and I where close enough to talk about his son.

"Yeah," I said. "He was telling me before you came in that he was worried about his son being sent up the creek. He came in early wanting to know what I could tell him to tell his son about what to do when he got inside."

Leroy just froze, checking my face.

"You're sure you heard that right, son?"

"Absolutely," I said without a doubt. "I always heard about your sons and that other brother's son, but I never heard about his son or sons."

"That's because Joe doesn't have a son, son."

"Huh?"

"Joe doesn't have a son. In fact, in all his messing around I'm amazed that he hadn't had some woman pinning a child or child support on him. I just well enough assumed that his plumbing wasn't right down there. Our cousins and 'em used to do a number on him back then."

Leroy went onto explain that the reason why Joe didn't get along with most of the family that came into work was because they were usually the children of their first cousins whom he really couldn't stand. Who were the children of their aunts and uncles that Leroy and Joe were forced to stay with after their parents went their separate ways. "My cousins were some badass kids. They resented Joe and me when we were younger because we were more blessed when it came to the girls, if you know what I mean." He said somberly. "Joe was a lot smaller then. He couldn't defend himself like he can now. Not like I could. He took a lot of hits to the balls because some easy girl was making a big to-do about our...uh, you know."

I didn't know what to make of it. Joe was telling me that he was worried about a son that was imaginary. My boss, Leroy, was finally coming around to trusting me but he wanted me to baby-sit his younger brother. Plus, he was laying a bit of their family history on me.

Leroy talked me into riding out with Joe for the day. Although I wasn't keen on babysitting him, I was still a subordinate and doing my job was still in the confines of my work. I didn't bust him out on his lie and couldn't figure out what he had to gain from lying to me. The only thing I could think of was that it was somehow tied to Willie and the day before. How?

The day whizzed by like usual and I got back to the house just a couple of hours shy of midnight. The house was pretty much emptied out except for Calvin and Willie, who chose to stay behind after the rest of them headed out to some sort of thing. House? Ball? J-Set? Club? Something? And even Calvin wasn't sticking around, making his way downstairs to the basement to see what college-aged scraps he could find to get into.

I was tired. It wasn't the kind of tired that made me want to hit the hay. I wanted to do something. What that was exactly I hadn't the foggiest of ideas. I thought about calling up my other pieces, but I then looked over at Willie aimlessly walking by. I wasn't thinking about getting with him. Instead I was more interested in asking him to join me at a nearby bar for a drink. He agreed, putting a smile on my face and the wheel in motion. It didn't occur to me until after I ask that maybe I could get him tipsy enough to spill the beans about whatever led to the tension the day before. Unfortunately, we sat down in front of the television and never got up.

"They didn't say when they would be back?" I looked over and asked, laying back deep into the couch.

"I doubt with as many of them together we won't see them until about morning."

"I thought they cut the club hours?"

"Here, but not out in the suburbs," he said matter-of-factly. "And I wasn't even figuring that in. I was thinking that afterwards that they might hit up some after-hours spot to hang out at or get something to eat or something. Why?"

"Lazy. I figured if Priscilla was coming through that door in a minute that she could fix me something to eat."

"There some chicken tender in there." He said.

"The key emphasis was *she* could fix me to eat. But I guess I'll have to do it in a minute."

A sitcom rerun passed before I saw Willie get up off of the sofa. I didn't think much about it until he started shouting from the kitchen, "You want some French Fries with that?"

"Hell, yeah, thanks man."

"No problem," he said opening up the microwave. "You made me kind of hungry talking about food."

It ran for a couple of minutes and he returned to the couch with a big plate of chicken tenders and French fries that looked like two mountains.

"Damn, kid," I laughed. "I know that I'm a big man. If I ate that much I would never wake up."

"It ain't all for you." He smiled, gripping a fry and dipping it into this dish of ketchup before putting it in his mouth.

As I reached forward for tender strip, Willie jumped up off the sofa. I heard him tear a couple of sheets of paper towels off the roll. He came back into the living room handed me off mine and headed back into the kitchen.

"What's your poison?" He shouted.

I knew that he probably couldn't mix a drink, my favorite being 150 proof and coke, so it was no point in asking.

"What you got in their?"

"Beer...domestic beer, foreign beer, exotic beer, lemonade—"

"Alcoholic?"

"Yeah, in pink, regular, and pomegranate," he rattled off.

"Gimme the pomegranate, I need some fruit," I laughed.

He came back into the living room with his beer and my alcoholic pomegranate, two each.

We drank and ate and talked. My mind was somewhere else when I felt his eyes look over at me. We I looked he tried hard to pretend like he was looking at the television, taking his time to look a little more believable every time I glanced his way. But his deep, calculated breathing kept on giving him away.

I knew the boy had a crush on me, though innocent, as far as I could see. It was practically a given that ex-cons that were fucked on a continuum had a tendency to be aroused by an intimidating size, an intimidating man. This was part of the reason why I never acted on it, thinking that it probably wasn't a real emotion as it was a real reaction, which was sort of hot too.

"What?" I asked, catching him unable to take his eyes off of me.

"Oh," he said, shaken out of his trance. "I was wondering why you hadn't come out of your uniform. Work is over and shit."

"This was the first place I landed.   It's bothering you or something."

"Naw," he shook his head. "I just know that if I got off of work, I would want to climb out of my clothes and get comfortable."

"You would like that," I joked. "Like my food, I told myself that I was going to jump into the shower in a minute. Wash away the day. I had no beef climbing out of this got-damn thing right now. I was just worry about your ass. The way you're about to have an asthma attack over there with me in just this I could only imagine what your scrawny chest might do if I showed you my undershirt."

"Shut up," he said.

I teased him, slowly looking over at him unbuttoning and unzipping my jumper, showing off a sweat-sticky tee shirt and the top of some printed boxers.

"You okay over there?" I asked a moment later. I was feeling great that the trapped heat from the day unhurriedly rolled off of my body.

"Yeah, I fine, dude. Stop tripping."

"You're the one tripping over there. You like what you see?"

"No," he said, turning his head in an entirely different direction.

"I know you're lying. Ain't nothing over there to look at. Besides, I know I got a nice body. I ain't no harm in admiring it or even touching it for that matter. It ain't like nothing is going to pop off up in here."

"You sure?" He said, letting his disappointment show in his face.

"Damn right," I said. "If I wanted your sweet ass I would've had it doggie-style a long time ago."

"I know." He paused. "You like those girlie boys. I ain't about to go out like that."

"I like anybody that's on the end of my dick when it spits."   I laughed.

"Really?" He seemed surprised.

"No doubt," I said. "I'm just with Priscilla because she knows how to take real good care of what I got. As for you, I know that you got in some action somewhere but that's because you've were turned out by some proper dude in the yard. If I was going to fuck you, I want to be the one doing it. Not that other man."

I thought he was going to get angry. He was going to fly off the handle, but he calmly looked at my stomach, and told me that "you're wrong. Shit happened in there, but I was never turned out. I just always loved a man's physique, especially when it's muscled up like yours. I can't even lie."

"So it ain't about the dick?"

"Nah, not for me," he smiled. "It's the God's honest truth."

He confessed that he was enamored with bodies like mine because he always wanted one. He studies bodybuilding and everything, going to get products that boasted to bulk him up. He cried that while he was fortunate enough to develop defined and functional muscles, his wiry frame still carried it off as he was just another skinny kid.

As he talked, I took off my shirt, showing him proudly everything he couldn't be with my thick massive frame. He was so lost in his words that he didn't even know that I had took his hand and placed it on my pierced nipple chest, moving it from tatted pec over to tatted pec. He was so nervous and scared that he didn't even know what was going on. The second he did, his hand started to shake and sweat a small creek. Once he saw that I was cool, he started rubbing on my cobblestone stomach like he was making three wishes. It took me a minute to realize that he wasn't rubbing my stomach as he was trying to give it a massage.

"Don't leave that other hand out, man." I said getting into the groove of it and the playing television.

He obliged.

The way he used both hands wasn't the same way he used his one. Maybe it had to do with how he was sitting or something, I don't know. I do know that it was ticklish as hell. I tried not to laugh until there was a funny moment on the television. His hands were going back and forth, back and forth, sometimes giving some extra attention to my diesel cut chest.

It should have come as no surprise when one of his hands started etching towards the top of my boxers below. But the way Willie was focused solely on my muscle groups gave me absolutely no reason to think otherwise, given what he said, even though I took it with a grain of salt originally. That hand was taking two steps forward and one step back before it danced over my sleeping dick.

He said nothing, and neither did I waiting on him to slip that hand in the slit and start playing with it, which he never did.

"You already woke it up so you might as well." I said, as his mouth magically found its way around my pierced nipple while tweaking the other.

"What if Priscilla comes back?"

"What if she comes back now? What am I going to say? Willie tripped and I thought it was best that I breast fed him before bedtime. Besides, you don't think you can take her? You're going to let some transvestite whup your ass?"

"I was worried about you." He said with his eyes smiling more than his mouth.

"Dick quiets the soul…and the lips." I said. "You can get down there and suck it."

"What about Calvin, man? He's right downstairs?"

"He ain't studying what's going on. He's getting ass like you should be getting on this dick."

"Like I said, I ain't about the dick as much as I'm about that body."

"That ain't what Joe said." I said, meaning to say Mack where I said Joe.

"He told you?"

"Yeah," I lied, feeling like I was opening a new chapter in this story. "He came in early just so he could spend the day telling me ever filthy detail."

"He just got in where he could fit in." Willie said gravely.

It was deep the way he was talking, and I was too much in the mood to play psychologist next to my lust. I slid off the rest of my jumper and threw my arms behind the couch as he got in position between my widely spread legs. I waited patiently on him as he fished out the growing one-eyed monster from the slit of my boxers.

"What you going to do with it?" I asked calmly with him holding the tip end of the shaft. "What're you waiting on?"

He hesitated. He wasn't like most guys, though, intimidated by my size. He looked like he was savoring the moment, and with his mouth wide open it turned me on even more because I knew then that this wasn't going to be some rush job, if we could help it.

"You've gotten that close. Stick your tongue out. Lick that pearl drop off the tip." I said even calmer.

He wrapped his hand around my thick piece of uncut meat and gradually started stroking it, egging me to pull my boxers down as well.

"Do the damn thing." I coached, exhaling, getting lost in those smooth sensual strokes.

Willie jutted out his tongue. He took a hard lick at the exposed mushroom head. He teased the piss slit with his sandpaper of taste buds, and preceded to slowly started to draw me in, sucking me like a straw. He wasn't quite sated until he had my dickhead pressed against the roof of his mouth. I tried to let him take it from there, let him find his groove, relax that throat of his. But my animal instinct was impatient, taking the back of his head and ever so graciously guiding it down so he could take more of me in his mouth.

"It was the God's honest truth, huh?" I laughed, reminding him of what he said earlier.

He didn't care. He was as a happy as a clam with his mouth full of dick, his heavy drool strolling down to my balls. I knew he wasn't going to get it all down, just because of how big I was, but I was amazed how much he gobbled down given our position. Willie gave both Priscilla and the drug dealer a run for his money, the way his tongue was ripping around the shaft while I was grazing the back of his throat.

"Damn, son," I mouthed. "They taught you well...whoever that was."

He mumbled something. The next thing I knew was that he was giving my large ball a nice squeeze that for the first time in a long time sent a jolt through me. The second time he did it, the way he did, I thought I was going skeet some nice cream into his mouth. I was fighting the feeling so hard that I didn't even feel his bony finger bump up and around my sweaty bunghole.

He took his time, proceeding with caution. He was trembling on the other end of me waiting for me to jump up and beat his ass. If I didn't, he knew I was cool. What he didn't know was that I was good. Though I never got fucked or finger fucked, I wasn't above getting my hole eaten out. I got into it years earlier when I was dating this freak that had a thing for man-ass. She touched it, played with it, and even stuck her tongue up there to get a taste of the "scent". And after I started seeing in some selective heterosexual porn, I didn't think much of it as taboo.

"You want to eat some ass, huh?"

He mumbled.

"Only if I get some ass from you next," I said patiently. "You think you can handle what I got back there?"

He mumbled again.

"Good," I said. "Work your way down to the balls, get that spot in between there, and go in for it."

He obliged, meticulously taking every step I told him before I had my ass rolled up off the couch just enough so he could use his tongue right there.

"Lick that shit." I commanded.

He parted my ass cheeks. I was expecting him to just dart his tongue in and out, but he didn't. Instead, he kissed it, puckered up as if he was kissing somebody on the lips before deviling into French kissing. Much like my dick, he did it in a round circular motion that I had me groaning and tugging at my dick.

"Damn that shit feels good! Damn that tongue." I told him.

He picked up the tempo and started going at it. He was licking my asshole like he was he was going spoon-less in a yogurt cup, nothing but fast wet tongue. I was moaning and groaning against that tongue like it was best thing I felt next to busting a nutt.

I hated to admit that I was being had, but he had me eating right in the palm of his hands. I wasn't going to let him get away with it, though. With my dick in hand, I jerked it for dear life. I felt my balls retract, my licked hole twitch, and with my dick pointed, primed, and swollen I shot a nice pint of smoking hot cum straight up into the air, hitting the back of his head. I was sure that I got some on the back of his neck and beyond.

I was sure that Willie knew something happened, but wasn't sure what. He pulled his head from my ass. He looked around and saw that there was nobody around, I grabbed his head and shoved it back onto my crotch.

"Clean your shit up." I berated him.

He brought me down with the same skill and vigor that he did eating my ass, getting up in that slowly covering foreskin.

I just chucked it up to that talented tongue.

I got up, sprayed the room deodorizer, and hopped in a nice hot shower.

■■■

After I got to bed, I thought about what Willie said. All the stuff that I wasn't paying attention to when I knew I could get him on my dick. The way he made it sound, he had more to do with Joe than he did with Mack. The more I thought about it the more it made sense. Mack was always mean-mugging somebody, so he probably wasn't even apart of the equation to begin with.

I slept pretty good and got up invigorated. I went to work hoping to catch Joe alone again and bluff him out of his story. Unfortunately, it turned into the same old same old, with the exception that Leroy went out with Joe and I got stuck with Mack. That didn't mean that I still couldn't fish out any information. I was glad to know that I was right though, and that Mack hadn't a clue of who Willie was other than the dude that stepped in there with me. He did startle me in knowing that Priscilla was my girl and that I was her man. He seemed heavily disappointed that I alluded to the fact that the relationship was a go-between for me.

The next day however I got a chance to work with Joe. I felt that I had enough ammunition to call him out, given what I already knew. Yet, there was this subdued feeling that told me I needed to let everything play itself out. Let everything come to a head and reveal itself. The way went off without much fan fare, and. It was about eleven o'clock at night before we pulled into this overnight dive for a late dinner. We sat down, got our drinks, ordered, and I headed off to the bathroom, not knowing that he wasn't far behind me. I didn't think anything of it. I had to go. He probably had to go, too. It didn't become a problem until he stood in front of the urinal right next to me. This wasn't working, I thought. Two big guys, wide guys like us, standing side by side like that left little maneuvering room for either of us to do our thing. Thinking that there should have been a third urinal that he could've scooted over to use, I just happened to look over that way.

My ego was still freshly bruised from a few night back, after being with Willie. I was feeling slightly embarrassed that the "Proud Top" that I often boasted I was got off on a tongue playing in my ass. I had my ass eaten out plenty of times before. It was just in the realm of foreplay, never the main course. My ego felt like it was getting battered again when I looked over and saw it dangling over the toilet. I thought I had some ridiculously big dick. Once I saw his, I discovered that I didn't even know the meaning of the word was. Whereas mine was a generous forearm, his was a baby elephant trunk.

Maybe it was childish, but I was feeling real pain in that instant. I always knew that it was possible for a man to be bigger than I was. I just never came across any of them until then. I may not have always been the biggest guy in the room, but I took the world's greatest confidence in having the biggest penis most people had ever seen. But I could only imagine the jealously they might have if they knew something like that existed.

Before then, I never had an iota of an issue about my size. I showed off in the locker room, naturally thinking I was blessed in being height *and* weight proportionate to my dick that was long and thick. It was obvious Joe Bishop was too, standing there at six-eight. But still. It was sort of like a bad car accident about to happen. It was something that shouldn't be seen, but if there is a front and center seat its something that can't be missed, if you tried. It was so freakishly big it looked cartoonish, especially the spaceship-like head and the triple thick stream of piss that it emitted.

He snorted, snapping me back into my consciousness. I shook off the last bit of urine from the tip and started to put it back in my pants. I stopped shy of doing it. I had to take one more look. I don't know why, but it was something I had to do.

"I'm starting to see why Willie wouldn't talk." I accidentally mumbled.

Joe looked over at me looking down at him.

"Don't worry. I've gotten it all my life." Joe chuckled.

"Me, too," I laughed nervously, showing him mine.

"I take it that your boy told you how I split his sweet asshole with this thing?"

I shook my head. "He wouldn't talk. I just knew that your nephew never even heard of him."

"Yeah," Joe smiled. "You ever got some of that throat?"

"Yeah," I smiled which caused Joe to laugh.

"He got a nice one don't he?"

"No doubt, no doubt," I said emphasizing. "That tongue's on point."

"You got some of that ass, too?"

I shook my head again. "Throat was all I could handle. I felt like a sucker that came in his pants during a lap dance."

"Try it when you get the chance. If you thought the throat was the shit, try the back end. He got some good ass. I don't know about now but he used to serve it up like a ho. He used to be my bitch at a boarding house I used to manage."

So he was the infamous bully that Calvin was talking about, I thought.

"Everybody knows that tight ass and big dick is a lethal combination. He cried that folk raped him on the regular, which is why I ain't doing that no more. Yeah, I took it but I didn't rape his fruity ass. That bitch stayed on his back with those legs spread and that hole on grease. I just slid right on in. Pow!" Joe continued, thrusting his hips forward with the tip nearly crashing into the urinal.

"That ain't sliding man." I defended. "That's a wreck."

He laughed, slapping me on my back and looking down at me.

"Shit. You probably right. The way I see it, it takes one to know one."

"I don't do too bad." I said, grabbing at it.

"You got a nice piece man. Ain't too many that can be a little brother to mine. You know what I'm saying?"

"Yeah," I paused.

He looked at me and my dick, and started going into a trance. I thought it was best not to say anything especially when I saw that he was stroking his snake.

"Man, you done took me back thinkin' about that good bitch. Want to help me rub one out right quick?"

"Here?"

"No, next year fool," he said sarcastically.

"You're crazy? Somebody might come in here and catch us."

"Who? Ain't nobody comin' in here? And if they do, what they gonna do? You should know by now that nobody fuck with dudes our size."

He was right. People thought a lot of stuff, but rarely say anything to the effect fearing that our intimidating size spoke more than any words or authority could.

"It ain't nothin' like jacking off with a buddy," he encouraged.

I didn't say a thing. I just turned in his direction and slapped my dick against his, not believing that I was going to go through with this openly in a public restroom of a restaurant.

He grabbed his dick. I grabbed mine, listening to him tell me that we got to be quick with it since I was scared like a little punk. He was joking, but being the man that I was I couldn't let that go without a comeback. I let him know that he was the punk wanting to me jack off with him so that he could take a good look at my dick. We got into some heavy shit talking before we eventually grew quiet and simply started stroking. My hand automatically moved up to my nipples as his moved underneath my nutt sac. I reciprocated putting a nice sinister smile on his face. I thought I would take it to the next level by forcing our dicks to kiss a wet and sloppy mess.

The heat of our dicks touching and him pulling hard at my other nipple drove me over the edge. I winced, sucked my teeth and shot into his pubes. I was in the middle of catching my breath when he leaned forward and kissed me. I pinched his nipples and tried kissing him around his neck, noticing that those extra five inches in height were easier on him than they were on me.

A few minutes later, his soft groan was the extent of what I heard before I something warm and wet hit my thigh through my jumper. I later found the rest of it sat on top of my right boot.

"Toldja," he panted, tucking his dick back in his pants.

I hated to admit it, but he got me with that kiss. It wasn't like it was lovey-dovey or a poor imitation or something like that. It was a sensual masculine kiss that was only meant for what we did, but rarely did it feel like that.

Like a dumbass, I was sort of expecting another one for the road, but he said, "Let's get out of here. Our order is probably ready by now."

He led and I followed him out.

We sat and ate and talked as if what happened in the bathroom never even went down.

■■■

A couple of months passed by and Joe and I pretty much worked together almost every other day. He never mentioned a peep about that night, and neither did I. It was like if either one of us gave it too much thought we were putting more into it than it was. We would have been several sessions deep if we hadn't fucked up by kissing each other, turning a hot wholesome jack off into something questionably more.

But I was still good, though. I was having a ton of sex on the regular with just about anybody I could get my hands on. Though, I was more partial to those that generously donated to my sexual drive. Now that I was in the system, building my credit and had opened a checking and saving account, I didn't want to use my hard-earned money to party and bullshit. So it was only logical that I partied and bullshit with the extra that I got from whomever. My renewed burst of energy came from the fact that my tension level had dropped considerably since my first day on the job. The job was still taxing and stressful as ever. The thing was, because it wasn't as new and found my stride it made everything else a bit more digestible.

Especially when I went from the bottom to the top, being that I was the only one in the office that Leroy actually trusted.

And it wasn't it was weird between me and Joe either. Not that I knew of. He still talked a strong line of pussy, throwing in Willie and some of the other guys he knew from around the way that were known to mess around. He tried not to go too deep, but gave me enough of a heads up so that if I felt they were worth trying to pursue, I could pull their Ho Card if they started acting salty.

Then one Friday afternoon, Joe and I came back to the office super early to call it a day. It was the start of a three-day weekend, and we were planning on taking full advantage of it. Leroy was gone because his wife had convinced him to take her out of town. And Maggie wasn't around because she knew that Leroy wasn't going to be around. So that just left me and Joe.

Although we were too lazy to continue to work, it was still too early for us to do anything else. We thought we were smart by stopping over at a local barbershop, hoping to kill some time. Even with getting our haircuts, shooting the shit with some of the other fellas there, *and* playing a few board games, we still had a ton of time on our hands. His problem was that most of his womenfolk were most likely at work or running errands. Much in the same spirit as some of my other fuck buddies. There wasn't much for me to run home to either. While I was guaranteed an almost quiet and empty house, I wasn't about to run the risk of some lonely lovesick teenager attempting to monopolize my precious time.

The best either of us could come up with was to sit around the kitchen table and talk. We always talked. There wasn't really a workday that we didn't. The thing was our conversations circled more around the superficial than the two of us getting to know one another as two grown men. I don't think neither one of us were looking for a *Golden Girls* moment, but seeing that we had so much in common it seemed sort of sad that we weren't better acquaintances.

Without effort, he talked about his life in detail, touching on some of the stuff that Leroy had talked about throughout the months and some stuff that I would have never even known, given that we had never had that opportunity. I shared a few things with him about my life, too. When it was all said and done, we lightened the mood with our favorite subject talking about sex. I won't even lie. Talking about some our most memorable conquests nearly got us caught up like we did that night at the restaurant with a soft grope between two clothed buddies.

We stopped shy of getting started again. Joe received a call from Mack who had a line on a few women that were ready and willing. He asked Mack if it was cool if I could tag along. He saw no problem with it. But I told him to go ahead, I had other plans and I would lock up now that I had a key of my own. Joe left, and I headed upstairs to drop off the key to the truck.

I placed the truck key on the table where Leroy could easily find it come first thing Tuesday morning. I hadn't been anywhere near that room since that day I caught him jacking off that time. Because I still had some time on my hands before my evening got underway and I was fully alone, I thought I would kill some time feeding my curiosity by snooping around to find out what else my boss did in that room.

It was set up like a cheap efficiency that ran the length of the squat building. There was a small table next to this stub of a kitchen unit that ran along the opposite wall of the entranceway. On the other end of the room, there was an oversized couch facing the empty windows out into the street next to a raggedy recliner facing a relatively new television which sat at the foot of the cot. This, along with large and small storage containers littered in between. The large containers were filled with clothes and blankets and some other work-related stuff. The smaller containers were filled with basic necessities and other knickknacks.

Apart from the lack of space that crowded that side of the room, it still remained very much clean and organized. I tried to keep in mind that he was very much ex-military. The problem that I kept on running into was that even for him it was too clean and too organized for measly junk. Like there was this strange feeling that something needed to be hidden in plain sight. Just in case. The dilemma that I was running into was, was it any of my business to find out, being that I worked so hard to gain his trust? The obvious answer was no. I was a better man than I was a boy. When I did those things in the past I was going for things of monetary value to survive. There was nothing for me to acquire or get or get got from him that I didn't already have. That was, of course, minus the house and the business and it wasn't like I could hid them somewhere on my person. That was this gist of my old gig, I remembered. Get what I could get. At my worst I was at my best. No question. This—what I was going for—was pure curiosity. The risk was too high for so little if any reward. I had been away from the underside too long. I could mess up.

Then, the thing that always drove me kicked in, the excitement, the rush, the adrenaline. Yes, I was that good, or was, to try it without being detected. That was part of the fun back in the day. To do it in such a way that they didn't even know that their space had been violated until much later on.

Everybody was gone. I had a photogenic memory.

No.

I was halfway to the downstairs door when the itch got the best of me. I reasoned that I could at least wander around. Not touching the obvious and fumble around with things that weren't going to make much of a difference, starting with the television. I turned it on expecting to find it on some porno channel. The television only received air channels, which told me that the primary reasons that a fifty year old man used it were to play adult videos and catch up on the news. I was right. Hidden underneath the television was an expensive VCR-DVR player/converter. Beneath that was an array of porno flicks that failed to stray away from the typical babysitter fantasies and girl-on-girl action. At first glance, the original impression I walked away with was that it was something like his Top 25 favorites or something. The more I thought about it though the least likely that made any sense. The way they were hidden but displayed told me that those videos were put there with great forethought. In short, meaning that if somebody had gone that far to come across them, they were there to throw whomever off the scent. Given his paranoia, it made all the sense in the world. Where Leroy messed up was that none of his personality showed up in any of those flicks. It could've been his thing, don't get me wrong. However, Leroy was too much of a black empowerment kind of man to have such a lilywhite collection given the state of black porn. Next to that, those videos I saw in that cabinet were too tightly in there, leading me to two connecting but different conclusions: 1) it gave the impression that there were some more somewhere else in spite of the fact there was room to stack them on top of or around the existing collection, and 2) it was almost next to impossible to pry the tapes he had down there, telling me that it was some of the stuff he least watched.

Something told me to turn on the machine and change the channel to either Channel Three or Four, and there it was. It was an amateur-made-for-porn featuring a four blinged-out black guys taking turns spraying their loads in the face of a submissive white suburban housewife. Her husband soon comes home angry to find the men surrounding his wife and threatens to call the police. They leave, and once he gets his wife alone he licks her face clean of cum.

I knew there had to be more films like that. Nobody started off on amateur without growing tired of the professional-grade stuff unless it was homemade. I rumbled through the obvious stuff in the obvious places like under the bed or next to the nightstand, hoping that it would lead me in the right direction. It took awhile. Pulling stuff out and putting stuff back in the same spirit I found them, but I stumbled across the mother load in several large containers stacked on top of one another each hidden thinly under some thick work pads. It wasn't until after I found them that it made sense that was where they would be. They were sort of the odd containers out in the room and ones that were quite accessible to the television and the player to change in and out on a whim.

When I said I hit the mother load, I hit the mother load. He probably had every straight black porn and compilation ever made. And that was not including the boatload of interracial stuff that featured black men and a rainbow coalition of women of other ethnicities. I was tempted to grab a few of the videos, but thought it was best not to push my luck. I engrained the faces and titles to mind, in hopes of renting a few of them out later on down the road. I thought I was impressed with his library until I came across a couple of black gay titles featuring these muscled-up black guys on the cover of a bootlegged black and white. These weren't like Bobby Blake or Flex-Deon Blake or anything like that. These were like freakishly muscled up he-man giants that made them look average. I had never seen them before, and was thrown that the cover boasted something about Senegal and Guinea, West Africa. I was so aghast by cover that the fact that it was gay and that my boss owned it didn't even enter my mind.

I popped in the tape and was immediately blown out of the water. It jumped right into the night action with torches lit around this rock-ring of dirt with a large boulder in the middle. On it were these large thick mitts belonging to this nutbrown-colored muscled man bracing himself as a blue-black colossus mounted him doggie-style, and pounded away at him with what I can only describe as a greasy third thigh. The quality wasn't all that great but that was almost easy to forgive. The chocolate mountains of muscled men and the man-fucking they did with their overfed serpents was so raw and so intense and so hardcore that it made most of the best-intentioned muscle fuck studios feel like a total rip-off.

I was lounging back in the recliner ready to fist fuck a second load when I was startled by the presence of two angry eyes burning the side of my head. And before I could say anything this explosive voice shouted, "What the hell?"

It was Leroy.

Once the blood rushed back through my body, I jumped up and closed up my jumper halfway.

My next reaction was to cuss him out. He was supposed to have been far away on vacation with his wife. What the hell? I wasn't that cool, though, stumbling to find my words as he moved closer in on me.

He was already an ugly son of a bitch, but his anger showed me what ugly could really look like. He was ready to blow a gasket with his hands balled up in a fist ready to fight. I've been to prison and ran up on a few close calls, but never in my life was I as scared as I was in that moment. I should have been able to find my words quicker, if I knew what upset him most. The invasion of privacy or finding out he was the owner of one of the best porns I had ever seen.

I had to come up with something quick before we got into it. I won't say that the odds were against me. I was still a man and would fight hard to the end, which was part of the reason that I didn't run though I was quite sure that I could outmaneuver him.

"I-I-I-I thought that I would come up here to put the keys on the table. When I got up here I thought I would turn on the television to catch some news before I left." I lied, but felt it was coming off as believable. "I turned it on and it was frozen to some flick. I was getting ready to turn it off when I came across a flick I thought I would like."

"Yeah, but that flick wasn't in there." He said, still in hard stance, walking me around the room as the grumble and roars seemed to grow louder to fill the space.

"I know. I know. When I came back up from squatting down, I tipped back and knocked the containers over. I was so busy trying to make sure that everything was okay that I came across. I saw that it wasn't like the rest. I popped it in and got caught up."

"You had no business." He stopped, giving me more time to think.

"You're right. You're absolutely right. I'm sorry." I agreed.

"Forget it." He mumbled.

"Where did you get it?"

He gave me a nasty look and asked, "You gay or something?"

I could've come back with something hard, but chose not to. With most black men there was a world of difference between being gay and messing around with another man, and although I had pulled him back from the edge he was still relatively close to it.

"I got plenty action back when I was locked up."

"Yeah," he said softly.

"Pussy is great when it's soaking wet. Like a slip 'n' slide. But a good tight ass will choke the life out of a dick."

"You don't say?" He smiled.

"Don't it look your boy is having the time of his life?" I said, looking back at the television with another giant growling and practically doing pushups on his smaller but beefier counterpart. "I bet back in the Service there was some cocksucker that took care of the barracks. He probably had some good ass that you remember, too."

I could tell that I struck a cord.

"He only sucked my dick. And he only gave me that ass one time." He defended.

"It was good wasn't it?"

"Hell, yeah," he smiled. "If my wife—when she was my girlfriend— wasn't pregnant with my firstborn, I probably would've high-tailed it with him to San Francisco or something."

"It was that good, huh?"

"Yeah," he said.

"I know that you've gotten some ass since then?"

"I've had a season or two," he said to my surprise. "Back when I was younger, of course. I got that video about fifteen years ago during my last rendezvous. As I got older I realized that Mary's been good to a man with a face like mine."

"Man, stop that shit." I said moving slowly closer to him. "What you lack with that mug you damn sure make up for with that body of yours."

"Really," he said mockingly.

"Hell, yeah, no lie, Leroy," I replied in a deep and husky tone. "I can't believe that I'm going to say this, but shit, there been a few nights I've jacked off thinking about all that tight body of yours. For some damn reason, it makes for some nice eye candy in spite of the face."

"Really," he said assured.

"Yeah, in fact, it took me awhile to realize that the face is actually a nice part of the package. By no fucking means are you a pretty boy, but is sort of brings everything together. Like you need a hard face for those hard muscles or some shit like that."

I saw the wheel spinning in his heard. He looked at me in a way that made me feel totally uncomfortable. There weren't a whole lot of men that did that to me. There weren't a whole lot of men that did it for me either. Even when I thought I knew my type, I was discovering that I didn't. He didn't even come close to the profile that I thought. But everything I said before was true. I was very much attracted to him. I just didn't know what I was going to do with it.

It was one thing when I simply wanted to fuck somebody. The answer was simple. I found a way to coax them into a position where that was viable. This was virgin territory for me. I was extremely attracted to a man whose ass I didn't want fuck yet still had an undeniable lust for. Along with the fact that it was blatantly obvious that I was dealing with a man that didn't get fucked no how. I could've rolled with the punches, suppressed the butterflies in my stomach, had I been in that position before, to weigh in on the experience. But I hadn't. The thought never really crossed my mind. As far as I knew I was a big man with a big dick therefore the rules were set in stone. I automatically got ass or at a minimum was a wingman during the affair. The dilemma that I was facing was that Leroy was an even bigger man. If he was anything like his brother, he had a bigger dick too. So, according to my rules, he got privileges, everything was stacked in his favor including his fifteen year seniority over me.

"I got some gel and some cream lube stuff over there in the corner." Leroy nodded.

I was about to go through with it and my mind wasn't even in the room anymore. It had gone back to months earlier when I warned Joe about life behind bars.

Half the battle was lost when a man let it in his mind.

Leroy sniffed out my hidden desire.

"Cool," I responded, getting my mind wrapped around this new concept. He was the predator and I was the prey. "Go get it."

It wasn't so much as coming up against a man that I thought was man enough to climb on my back. There were too many men over the years, in my past that I could have filled that void. It finally occurred to me that if I was going to ever go through with it, I wanted my first to be the one I felt I had every right to submit to. He was the first if not the only authority I had to answer to in my adult years. I usually made the rules as I went. If I didn't like what was said, I let it be known, damning all the consequences. Leroy was somebody I had to answer to, came hell or high water. He was somebody I had no choice but to respect. Most importantly he was somebody's respect I had to genuinely earn, brick by brick and step by step. He couldn't be bent on that. It was a revelation that I even could. Even more devastating it was done without even known that I was doing it, without my conscious consent. In one careless instant, he let me know that respect was all we had in one another and I came this close to feeling the wrath of his intimidation.

I flinched for the first time in my life. I was scared of a man, a mature black muscled-bound macho man that was both tall and superb.

I was frightened, and when I recovered I was horny as hell.

I won't say that everything happened so fast because it didn't. That was most certain thing I remembered about that evening. The rest was slightly shard and blurred right up to that point. I can't remember what came first: the shucking of all our clothes or being on that couch. I do remember sitting down there. I wasn't getting on that cot. It was too damn close to those windows. It was the only control of my nerves that I had left. I remember him getting the lube and stuff, and putting it to the side. He sucked my dick first, in an attempt to get me relaxed. He told me that I was a beautiful man and that I was blessed with a beautiful piece. I remember that distinctly because I was lying back on the couch with him between my legs curious to see his.

We moved into a sixty-nine position. He was on top of me. And though I had his unforgiving dick in my not-so-willing mouth, I had a warped view of it with his heavy musty balls pressed against my nose. I was fighting so hard to breathe around the part that I could get into my mouth that I wasn't brought into the new until I felt a warm wet finger slide scrupulously in and out of my hole. It didn't hurt. It just made me wince with a tinge of discomfort that I didn't worry about. I was certain that my body was going to reject the foreign object, much like many tight asses that weren't ready to give in. I guess I was one of those rare exceptions. The more his meaty digit came into me the more it welcomed him and the tenderness against my mental will. I was deathly afraid of more invaders, even though I was fully aware what was about to go down soon.

He stopped shy of slipping in another finger. Thank goodness, I thought lamely. We broke away from our sixty-nine position, and he was on the other end of me licking the soles of my big-ass feet, size sixteen. I thought nothing of it other than he had a thing for feet. Stranger fetishes had happened to stranger people. Whatever got his goat. He worked his way from licking the soles to sucking my toes, starting with the baby toe and gradually worked his way back up. Once he got to that second toe next to the big toe, my body started to convulse and a sound that I didn't know I could make came out of my grit-teethed mouth. The next thing I knew I felt my butthole gape open. The experience was so new to me that I didn't know what to make of it.

Leroy did. Unfazed, he just kept on sucking my toe watching me go spasm beneath him. It was like I was torn between desperately wanting him to stop and pressed to see where it would lead. Forever had passed, it seemed, and I no longer had control of my own body. My sensory was in overload and there wasn't shit I could do. I couldn't even pry my foot away from his mouth.

After a long while, I came back to where he tugged firmly on my balls bringing them down to around my hole as he fingered it once more. It accepted him more willingly than before. He painstakingly put it in and painstakingly pulled it out. When he put it in again, I found it odd that his finger was remarkably softer than it was the first time. It took me a second to accept that it was softer because it was wet. And it was wet because I was wet. Bastard! I wasn't bleeding. This was all-natural, a doing of my own from what he done to me.

We're going to have so much fun, his eyes smiled, knowing that he had me where he wanted me. Something in my mind told me to look down. I did, and my stomach nearly dropped out of my hole. I got a clear and unadulterated view of Leroy in all his glory. He had a massive uncut swinging dick that rivaled his brother but wasn't nearly as thick as it was long. I knew game and I respected. He needed me to get open just like I needed to get many of my pieces open.

"I don't think we really need this," he said, fingering the lube in my sloppy wet hole after fisting it on his dick. "But this here ain't no joke, son."

He pulled me closer to him by my powerful thighs. The length of his dick rode the groove my crack and then some. I snapped back into the fullest of consciousness then. He was too damn big for my first time.

Please, oh fucking please, reconsider! I'm too much of a man to run. I won't run. But you can reconsider it, everything. Aw, damn!

He lifted me off of him a bit, and I felt the greasy head of his pole hit just above my hole.

"Just relax," he warned.

It was easier said and done, thinking about the countless assholes I said that to and never showed mercy.

He was fucking with my head rubbing it up and down and around my hole sometimes rubbing on it just for fun. He took my foot back in his mouth. It gaped open and he just sunk it in there.

He was enormously big, but it felt surprisingly soft like a rolled up taco was being shoved in my hole. It hurt, but not nearly as bad as I thought.

He let go of my foot and let it drop to his side. He brought my ass back down on him. Centimeters felt like inches, inches felt like feet, and his foot long plus felt about a mile long down to the hilt.

"Ah, shit," he groaned the way a man took a much needed piss.

I was feeling so much in one moment that it was hard to start with just one feeling. For the first time in my life, I was on the other end of one biggest dicks I had ever seen. I had an inkling into the world of all the bottoms I had ever fucked. I felt full, shot with a speeding hot bullet, split wide open and the pressure that his dick went well passed by bellybutton. Yet, in spite of this, I remained relatively calm exhaling deep, thinking back to what I told myself years ago if this had gone down in prison.

He pushed all of it in me, and held steady like letting me know that this was how much of my guts he was going to ream out. He pulled back. The first few lunges were annoying as they were painful as they weren't as deep. It felt like something in me was slowly closing up. I got the reason why when he started to thrust deeper into me. He was knocking the wind out of me. My head felt like it was about to explode with his dick coming through it. It felt like it was also floating away at the same time. I tried not to focus on the godforsaken pain because there was a small amount of pleasure in the mix every time he stroked passed my prostate.

This must have read well on my face because he upped the ante by literally lifting me off the sofa with every killer pump. I wouldn't have believed it if I heard it given my weight and size. Leroy was a mad man with it. I had to reach back and brace myself against the arm of the sofa so that I didn't fly off the edge.

I wanted to scream, tap out. But he man inside of me just bit my tongue and grunted like a pig led to slaughter, listening to his dick slide in and out of me farting like pussy.

I got lost in the action. The inside of my hole grew numb. The outside was growing even more sensitive to the entanglement of his pubes. I wanted to hold on this feeling while I was feeling it, so I gyrated back against him.

"Damn, if I knew that the ass was this good." He kept on mumbling from time to time.

He flipped me on my stomach, and brought my ass back to him doggie-style.

In this new position he made sure that I felt every inquiring inch with the eloquence and style a fine horseman parading around his prized stallion. I felt like a piece of meat before but this was new.

He got tired of this gentlemanly role and laid me back down. The position wasn't nearly as welcoming as the other two given our bodies and the softness of oversized couch.

He flipped me again, back on my back, where he regained his stride and plowed into me like a vicious monster. Though he had amazing stamina, he was getting tired and sweating while my butthole hurt and I was sweating over everything.

Eventually, I thought enough of him to pull him forward in for a kiss. He obliged keeping in mind that his first job was to take care of his dick with my ass.

He rode it this way.

I was feeling all kinds of something, waves of nutt-less orgasms every time he hit that spot. I couldn't take it any more. I always kept my hand on my dick. I just had it more or less to rub it than to jack off. Foolishly, I thought I was still holding on to something, a piece of my manhood, letting him know that I wasn't that easy.

I grabbed my dick and started jacking off. After only a few measly strokes, I popped a gusher-like wad that shot from my dick back onto my slick stomach. I was so embarrassed in moment that I immediately threw my draining dick back at his likewise cobblestone stomach, painting it white with cum.

Surely, I thought Leroy was right behind me. He had to be near the edge looking at that lake of cum that he drilled out of me. My hole was closing up and I was feeling more of him than I was before, which meant that he didn't have nearly the leeway he had before.

The old man had something to prove apparently. He was still pounding away long after the cum on his stomach had made its way down to his pubes and back to my balls before it got lost in sticky sweat. I thought I did everything to make him cum. I pulled at his nipples, gripped his butt cheeks, and pulled his balls, nothing.

I was about to punch him in his stomach as a last ditch effort when I felt his dick grow bigger inside of me followed by this steady stream of warm goo coating the hole that he fucked ever so raw.

Even after he came, he kept his dick up in my ass letting it crawl out naturally as he caught his breath. As the last of it came out, he wanted to start kissing and caressing on me like we had made love or something.

It wasn't fucking as much as it was sex, suddenly remembering why it couldn't be anything more than that. It was as clear as the writing on the walls. He was old-school. He was one of those men that only viewed it as cheating as long as he was with another woman. He simply saw our actions as another man helping out a friend with some affection in between.

"Man," he smiled. "That was great!"

"It was alright." I agreed, sounding like my usual nonchalant self, causing me to smile at this revelation that I was still the same old man.

"I'm not saying that this is something I want to keep up on the regular. I'm just saying that it would be *too bad* to have a buddy to watch a flick with from time to time...even if we do nothing more than jack off or something."

...

I left, and with every step I took I walked with him wet in my ass and dripping down my leg. I couldn't run home. I knew the scent of sex would roll off of me, and I was deathly afraid that I was going to tell on myself more than I wanted to. Since I always had an extra change of work clothes in my truck and knew where a full-service truck stop was on the outskirts of town, I drove out there. I threw my clothes into the washer and with some cleaning stuff in I jumped in the shower to wash off the evidence.

I had just finished vacuuming and spraying down the inside of my truck when I got a call from Mack invited me out to a strip club with him and his uncle. I usually rejected most of his invites. Even though I liked Mack as a man, it was quite obvious early on that we rolled in two entirely different circles. This time I agreed. I felt that if I headed home in the squeaky clean condition that I was in after being at "work all day" would have suggested that I was trying hard to cover something up. So I agreed.

I met up with Mack and Joe and a few of their other friends sitting in front and center. I took my spot next to them like I was still one of the guys. Minus the self-conscious feeling of recently having my asshole stretched. We drank and we smoked, and had a kick-ass good time. I ordered lap dances left and right. Right off the bat, most people might have thought that I was trying to cover up or compensate for recent events. But that couldn't have been further from the truth. I wasn't even bombarded with the self-impression of feeling like less than a man for getting fucked like I thought I should or would. The truth of the matter, I walked away from it a more gracious man, tipping those strippers extremely well as my way apologizing to every woman that ever took my big-ass dick with joyful abandon.

I understood now that it was hard work.

While my dick was in full swing giving my money away, Joe was off in the corner getting piss-drunk. At the time, I thought it had nothing to do with me until I was appointed his designated driver. He got so tore up that he was afraid for dear life to go home to his nagging wife. My first thought was to take him back to the office and leave him there. If Leroy was or wasn't still there, it was fine by me either way. Joe convinced me otherwise. He wanted me to drop him off at this new motel, to scout it out as a new place to bring the pussy he was bound to get. It was easier said than done. He may have had the money, but I was the one with the means of having to be the one to check him in. If that wasn't enough, unbeknownst to me, the motel clerk gave me a room in the back on the second floor. I thought because the place was so big in the front that the room wasn't that far away. It was one thing to have a sore ass posting up his hefty frame as we strolled through parking lot looking like two idiots. It was another having to stuff his drunken ass back into my truck once we found out there were rows of other buildings behind that main one. We rode around to eventually find the right building, take his sorry ass back out of the truck, and drag it up the stairs and into his room.

I was so tired that I was tempted to leave him right there on the ground in front of the room. My conscious started to kick in, and I thought the least I could do with the three hundred dollar tip he gave me was see him into the room and into the bed.

I was just about there, about to toss him on the bed, when out of nowhere Joe swooped behind me and locked his arms under mine and his hands behind my head.

"What the fuck is wrong with you?" I shouted.

I never been in this position before, taken by surprise like this. My large build had always protected me from any kind of foolishness.

"I want to fuck you." He whispered in my ear, very low and sexy-like.

The message became even clearer once I felt his dick point up again my clothed backside.

There were two things I thought I could do. If I was still the man from a few hours back, the one jacking off to a flick, I would've protested being that I never got fucked before. Maybe it was still a bit of the alcohol talking or the tiredness of lugging him around, but I figured that since I was still sore from when his brother stretched me out that I might as well finish off the night with him. Being that in my mind this was a one-night only sort of thing. Get now or get never.

"I want you to suck my dick."

"Yeah," he said hoarsely.

I moved my head against the back of his calloused hands. "Shit, I want you to take those pussy-eating lips and eat my ass, motherfucker." I mouthed.

"I knew you were down." He said with a devilish smile burning into the back of my head.

"I knew you were too." I said, thinking that he probably thought I got turned out in prison.

He slowly let go of my arms and started to fumble with the front of my jumper, coming out of it with nothing more than my underclothes and my boots. I didn't mind coming out of my undershirt and underwear. But I said to myself that if I was going to get fucked again I was going to make it even more memorable by getting fucked with my boots on.

Joe wasted no time tossing me on the bed. I was trying hard to hold in my laughter kneeing the bed with my legs spread and my strong arms holding the rest of me up. I couldn't believe that I was doing this shit again, I thought, going from never getting fucked in my thirty-five years to twice in one night. He pulled my dick from between my legs and into his mouth. He was just like his brother. He was no virgin to giving some head. Except that with his brother it was more of a formality and with him it was something that he truly enjoyed.

Joe took it in deep. He didn't get down to the balls but it felt like he got awfully close with my short curled hairs tickling against his nose. He thought he was being slick by thumbing around my aching hole, which was still wet from the shower earlier and the perspiration it collected from sitting at the club.

"Don't play with your food." I exhaled.

He took the cue and worked his way on up passed my balls and into my crack. I only *thought* he loved sucking dick compared to the way he pulled my cheeks apart and ate me out. I always knew I had a big bulky ass. I had too many people tell me that most of my life, and sort of knew it the way I poured into just about every pair of pants I ever wore. I just didn't know how big it was until my sculpted ass padlocked his entire face with it. This seemed to turn him on even more, eating it like it was about to be taken away. He got so lost in eating me out that I had to remind him that he said he wanted to fuck me too.

Once I got the words out, I started to regret what I said. I thought about his dick and the lube that I was sure that we didn't have with us. Even with the slob up in my hole it was bound to dry up after a few strokes. I couldn't get my words together fast enough before he was already positioned behind me pushing in that sick movie-sized anaconda into me. The slickness was surprisingly fine. It just didn't do much for the searing pain that was in my intestines that he was making worst with his kind of rub. I swore up and down that he had it down to the hilt until I felt his balls on top of my balls.

"Damn, son, you got one of those Hungry Hungry Hippo holes." He joked.

He pushed it in carefully but pulled it out with a vengeance. The pain was indescribable. It hurt like hell, knocking out any notion of wanting to laugh at my unusual situation, leaving me speechless. He stepped back for a second and threw something on the bed next to me. He resumed the position, throwing it back in there like he was tossing a football. It hurt still, but not as much causing me to let out this screech that I never heard in my life.

"Don't tell me that this dick is killing you the way it swallowed it up, now?" He smirked, grabbing me by my waist and manually stroking me on his dick. "Take it all in one stroke. Hoes can't even take it pro like that."

"Fuck," I groaned with him impaling me further on his dick, too tired and sore to add "you."

"You like big dick, huh? You like this dick, bitch?" He asked.

I was too busy catching my breath, trying cough up the words to tell him to take it easy and that I was on the verge of whupping his ass by calling me a bitch. A bitch got fucked, I thought. I had to instantly rethink that, quickly remembering my position. A bitch was one that liked to get fucked. I had to rethink that again too, seeing that I was getting fucked for a second time in less than a six hour period, and by his brother no less.

"Huh," he pounded into me. "Tell me that you like this shit. Yeah. Take it like you my bitch, bitch."

He fucked me for everything I was worth and then some. I tried every trick that ever been tried on me to get this over with, but nothing worked. He did however reach over me and jack me off. I came harder than I did before. He caught a good bit of it in his calloused hand and smeared hard across my mouth, trying roughly to work his fingers in my mouth. He got passed the lips but not the teeth. He was not going to spoon-feed me my nutt like I was some bitch in heat that didn't give a shit. Different from before, my hole didn't feel like it was locking around his dick. It felt oddly looser. This caused him to dig his fingers into me to get a better grip. I guess he got too great of a grip because while I was afraid of shitting I felt his ultra hot cum filling my guts.

"Oh," I hollered, feeling like shards of glass just exploded in my ass.

"Shut the fuck up and take it," the forty-eight year old said, gently sliding his softening dick in and out of my asshole. "I didn't even need the Vaseline for your ho' ass."

He gave me ass one last smack as he pulled out and fell on my back. He kissed me on my neck and told me that it was good, never knowing that it could be *that good.*

I left his words as I found them. I was too damn tired.

I fell asleep underneath him and about a few hours later dropping him off at his house, acting like nothing happened as we did before.

■■■

I came back to work the following Tuesday morning with my head held high. I won't even lie. I spent the entire three-day weekend debating if I was going to take an extra day off or if I was ever going to show my face at work again. It was bad enough that went from a proud alpha male to losing my butthole virginity to a man that could kick my ass, but it was a harder pill to swallow, to get over this slutty notion that I let two brothers that I work for bareback me. I had to remember though that I was still a man. I still had responsibilities and a driven purpose of legally showing the bank and the government that I had the means to buy a house. Astonishingly, there wasn't even a moment of uneasiness, and nothing much changed for the worst. Joe and I worked out a beautiful compromise spending part of our time working and the other part of the time chasing tail with Mack. We still fucked around, but not nearly to the degree anyone would think given the amount of time we spent together. We were too busy chasing around anonymous tail to be bothered. As for Leroy and I, we were cooler than ever. We hung out upstairs after worked watching one of his many flicks about every couple of weeks or so. We pretty much jacked off every time, with him stretched out on the cot and with me sitting on the couch. We probably got into something a bit extra about every other month or so.

I stayed with the job about a couple of years after that, long enough to show the system my W-2 forms. It was also long enough for Leroy and his other mysterious brother to come to their sense and allowed me to buy out Joe, after I made a few very profitable changes. Of course, the buyout subtracted a couple of percentage points so that the Bishop family could hold the majority stake in the business.

My motto is as long as it is putting a steady flow of bread in my pocket I'm good.

CHAT ROOM

NatBLKMascTop: Whoady! Gone to get me some pineapple juice and you kidnapped me?

PigBoiBottom: Finder's keepers. In virtual reality it's all fair in love and war.

NatBLKMascTop: Don't know you well enough to be in love, so we're at war?

PigBoiBottom: Yep. I thought with me having you tied up you up would've said it all.

NatBLKMascTop: You got me tied down to this rail thing in some leather harness and chaps…interesting.

PigBoiBottom: …with nothing else on but a hard-on.

NatBLKMascTop: It seems you've captured my essence.

PigBoiBottom: lol. So you're over their drinking pineapple juice and vodka?

NatBLKMascTop: Nope, just straight pineapple juice. I heard that it makes the cum taste sweeter. I like my boys to drink up!

PigBoiBottom: lol. I bet you do!

NatBLKMascTop: No doubt. Thought it's hard to find somebody to suck me until I come. It takes me a long while to do so.

PigBoiBottom: How long?

NatBLKMascTop: Why? Want to give it a whirl?

PigBoiBottom: I need to chew my meat for awhile before I take a sip on some pineapple juice.

NatBLKMascTop: Trust. You'll be chewing and gnawing on it a long while before a drop of pineapple juice will even dribble out.

PigBoiBottom: Oh, it's like that?

NatBLKMascTop: Damn skippy, skippy.

PigBoiBottom: So whatcha wearing?

NatBLKMascTop: My birthday suit. You?

PigBoiBottom: For real?

NatBLKMascTop: My birthday suit. I have to set Willie wild and free when I'm at home. Nah, seriously, I got on some jeans and a wifebeater.

PigBoiBottom: You beat your wife?

NatBLKMascTop: lol. Nah, it's the shirt. A tank top. You do know what a tank top is? lol

PigBoiBottom: Yeah.

NatBLKMascTop: Then, now you know what a wifebeater is.

PigBoiBottom: Why they call it a wifebeater?

NatBLKMascTop: How the fuck am I suppose to know. They just do.

PigBoiBottom: That sort of sucks.

NatBLKMascTop: Why do you call yourself PigBoiBottom? I thought rabbits go at it harder than pigs.

PigBoiBottom: Pigs are hungrier and greedier, and I like my men to be the same way, Nat?

NatBLKMascTop: Nat?

PigBoiBottom: Isn't that your name?

NatBLKMascTop: Nope.

PigBoiBottom: So what does the "Nat" stand for in your handle?

NatBLKMascTop: Natural as in Natural Black Masculine Top—there are a lot of imitators online and plus it alleviates asking about bedroom roles.

PigBoiBottom: I understand that.

NatBLKMascTop: I come to understand that a good fifteen minutes can be wasted on a conversation that should've never taken place. You know what I mean?

PigBoiBottom: Yeah. I wasted an hour on here the other day talking to this bastard that swore up and down that he was a top. He came through the door with helium heels.

NatBLKMascTop: LMAO. I don't mean to laugh, but I hear that a lot. Let me assure you that I'm 110% top.

PigBoiBottom: 120% would make me feel better.

NatBLKMascTop: That too. To be honest, my dick up in your ass would be the thing to make you really feel better.

PigBoiBottom: You know me so well.

NatBLKMascTop: So tell me a little bit about yourself?

PigBoiBottom: Stats?

NatBLKMascTop: You say tomato I say tomato. Other way around, or however that saying goes. It doesn't work to well on screen.

PigBoiBottom: No. I like your effort though. lol. About me…about me… I'm half-Mongolian and half-Vietnamese. I was born here, raised in San Fran, moved to LA for school and got a job shortly after graduation that landed me here in San Diego.

NatBLKMascTop: It sounds to me like you're an Asian-flavored man making his way down to the board for some muy caliente! What? Next stop Tijuana?

PigBoiBottom: Yeah, if they got what I'm looking for.

NatBLKMascTop: Oh. So what is it that you're looking for?

PigBoiBottom: Party and bullshit.

NatBLKMascTop: I can get with that. Since there is obviously a cultural difference between us on racial lines, let me ask you, how do you feel about the brothas?

PigBoiBottom: Love me some dark meat in my Asian-flavored ass, no lie. My last three serious relationships were with black men. I hadn't had one since I packed and left LA, though. Meanwhile, since I moved down here to San D I have found a brown brotha or two to mess around with from around the way.

NatBLKMascTop: Cool.

PigBoiBottom: Oh, I was forgetting the rest of my stats.

NatBLKMascTop: Okay, shoot.

PigBoiBottom: Standing at five-nine, I'm a cute and thick sporting a three-day beard and just recently shaved the hair off my head. And for most of the men that I mess around with they say for an Asian boy I got one hell of a badunakadunk.

NatBLKMascTop: Shit, I like that!

PigBoiBottom: Cool, cool. Everybody and their mama want to call me a cub. I ain't fat nor sloppy or a femme. I'm just a nice solid thick boy that got a metal keg rather than a six pack. With a few digital technicalities, I pretty much look like what you see in this virtual world.

NatBLKMascTop: Cool. I need my boys to have some meat on their bones makes for some serious cushion pushin'.

PigBoiBottom: lol. So tell me about yourself.

NatBLKMascTop: Just your "average" tall, beefy black man.

PigBoiBottom: You, average? I don't believe it.

NatBLKMascTop: Nah. I thought I would give a try though.

PigBoiBottom: Spill it.

NatBLKMascTop: If I toldja you wouldn't believe me. It would come off as bragging.

PigBoiBottom: Try me.

NatBLKMascTop: Okay. I'm six-three, two hundred and fifty pounds plus packing some nice body-armored muscles. As of late people have been split down the middle in wanting to say that I have a football player build and a wrestler's build (what's really difference?). Most people will also swear I live at the gym, but I don't. I simply got tired of the gym stalkers looking for some post-workout training. I'm a naturally muscled, beefy motherfucker. I have a tight flat belly, about a half dozen tattoos and several body piercing. I have a shaven-head, too.

PigBoiBottom: Sounds like my kind of guy? Into leather?

NatBLKMascTop: Come out of the womb with a codpiece and a bullwhip.

PigBoiBottom: Old Guard?

NatBLKMascTop: I know a good bit about it to respect the game. Pretty much, I go about my own rules. Not new guard, but my own style.

PigBoiBottom: Daddy?

NatBLKMascTop: Prefer Big Poppa.

PigBoiBottom: Big Poppa, eh? Not to sound like a total size queen but how big is Big Poppa?

NatBLKMascTop: Big enough, lol.

PigBoiBottom: C'mon.

NatBLKMascTop: Wouldn't believe me if I told you.

PigBoiBottom: C'mon.

NatBLKMascTop: Let's just say that it's not for the faint of hearts.

PigBoiBottom: I can respect that. So I won't be disappointed if I saw it.

NatBLKMascTop: A pig bottom like you wouldn't have any complaints. You'll be like that white girl in that Civil War movie 'you'll never go hungry again!'

PigBoiBottom: Is that right? Don't make any promises you can't keep.

NatBLKMascTop: I promise I won't write a check that your ass can't cash in handsomely.

PigBoiBottom: I can it 24/7, 365. The problem is that I don't' come across too many BIG deposits that can take me out of commission.

NatBLKMascTop: lol. I'll put you out of business AND run your sweet ass out of town. I got a big-ass boar of a dick.

PigBoiBottom: Big dick.

NatBLKMascTop: I thought that was implied. It is so big that the Post Office is considering giving it its own zip code.

PigBoiBottom: Usually, I'll dismiss that sort of bragging, but I got a funny feeling that you got a whale watcher's dick. lol

NatBLKMascTop: A whale wishes he had so much! I can't lie it's a pretty nice size. Though, I'm disappointed that Subway will only pay $5 for my foot long.

PigBoiBottom: Damn. Is it thick?

NatBLKMascTop: Very.

PigBoiBottom: Cut or uncut?

NatBLKMascTop: I got some serious foreskin, too.

PigBoiBottom: I like that right there. I always got to live vicariously.

NatBLKMascTop: You got some on here.

PigBoiBottom: Digital technicality.

NatBLKMascTop: You ain't missing anything. I was suppose to have been cut too; but whoever left so much it was like I never was. Then, too, I "grew" some more. I can take it or leave it, but cut pieces are obessed over it.

PigBoiBottom: Can you blame them? I'm getting hard just thinking about it!

NatBLKMascTop: I got a feeling that you were hard already.

PigBoiBottom: Who told you?

NatBLKMascTop: Whatcha wearing?

PigBoiBottom: My birthday suit.

NatBLKMascTop: For real?

PigBoiBottom: Almost. I got on a jockstrap so that…

NatBLKMascTop: What?

PigBoiBottom: Nothing.

NatBLKMascTop: Tell me. Tell Big Poppa. Don't be ashamed.

PigBoiBottom: Well, I got on a jockstrap so that while I play on this computer I can also control the speed of the vibrating bullet in my ass.

NatBLKMascTop: Disgusting! No, just kidding. I wish I was over there so that you didn't have to fuck with no toys.

PigBoiBottom: Yeah, but the real thing eventually gives out.

NatBLKMascTop: So do batteries, my friend, so do batteries. So you got a vibrator up your ass while talking to Big Poppa. I can't hate on having an introduction.

PigBoiBottom: Introduction?

NatBLKMascTop: Yeah, as it is warming up your big juicy badunkadunk for me.

PigBoiBottom: For you, huh?

NatBLKMascTop: Of course. Who else? lol (*wink*)

PigBoiBottom: Aren't you special?

NatBLKMascTop: Not yet. I will be when I crank up that vibrator and put it on full blast to see what it can really do!

PigBoiBottom: Level two is pretty much all I can handle sitting at this chair.

NatBLKMascTop: C'mon, I know you can crank it up a notch. I'll let you nibble the hell out of my extra skin.

PigBoiBottom: Chew, baby, chew.

NatBLKMascTop: Cool. Chew on it like a long lasting stick of gum…or like some good-ass fried chicken skin.

PigBoiBottom: lol. No doubt. Thought I should give you a heads-up, I'm not the best at giving brains. I do my thing. It's just that I sort of get carried away with having a dick in my mouth that I forget to do any pleasing.

NatBLKMascTop: Oh, no!!! I drunk all that pineapple juice for nothing!!!

Shit, I ain't too worried about it. Even if you were good at giving head, I am too big of a boy for you to take down the windpipe like that. But at least I can give you your propos for that knowing what you can and cannot do. As long as you keep your teeth at bay we should be good—on and off the screen.

PigBoiBottom: What the hell?!?!

NatBLKMascTop: Oh, while you were cranking up that vibrator getting that ass super wet thinking about me in chat, I found a way to create a second me to until the first me from that rail thing. I kidnapped you into another virtual room where I got you looking like something straight out of a Tom of Finland picture.

I started to hang you like you did me on that rail thing. Then, I remembered I'm a bit more original than that, so I hung you upside down. I had your legs spread-eagle tied to the ceiling along with your arms and nutts so it looked like you were set up in an invisible sling. One of the voyeurs in the room suggested that I bound your wrists together. The next logical choice was connect your wrists and nutts by a pulley. That way when you start pulling on your wrists you're also tormenting your beloved testicles.

Watch.

See how your mouth opened up so you can suck off my naked double while my leathered original take a crack at your whorish bubblebutt with my bullwhip.

Ain't nothing like squealing bacon-hole first thing in the morning!

PigBoiBottom: Oink.

NatBLKMascTop: Good little piggy.

PigBoiBottom: Good? Great! I'll try my best to take care of my Big Poppa.

NatBLKMascTop: That was the plan.

PigBoiBottom: Even if I just get a drop of that sweet pineapples juice on my tongue, I'll be in heaven.

NatBLKMascTop: I like your spirit.

PigBoiBottom: I think you'll like my ass, Pa. It's my speci-al-ity!

NatBLKMascTop: Damn, you got my dick hard waiting it.

PigBoiBottom: You were already hard weren't you, Big Poppa?

NatBLKMascTop: Of course! I won't deny it. When an Asian boi like yourself uses the word "badunkadunk" to describe his derriere it is definitely a turn-on.

PigBoiBottom: Badunkadunk. I got a badunkadunk. Asian boi with a bundunkadunk all for Big Poppa.

NatBLKMascTop: You got cam?

PigBoiBottom: Hell, yeah. My sound card is jacked up though, so I'll still have to type.

NatBLKMascTop: Damn, you're phyne.

PigBoiBottom: You're sexy as hell, too, Pa. I'm going to have to turn up this vibrator just to get off.

NatBLKMascTop: Can you swerve that camera down?

Man, that hole is shaking like it ain't got no business.

PigBoiBottom: Let me see that dick, Pa.

Damn, I see why you love it when they call you Big Poppa. That ain't no dick. That shit right there is a jackhammer made for those manholes in the streets. Good God!

NatBLKMascTop: Glad you like.

PigBoiBottom: Explain something to me. How do you walk with that thing?

NatBLKMascTop: One leg at a time. Besides, it doesn't always stay hard like this. I do have some control over it.

PigBoiBottom: Even soft it looks like it could be a nice noticeable basket. Picnic anyone?

NatBLKMascTop: It is. That's why oversize jerseys and sagging jeans come in handy.

PigBoiBottom: Trying to go for that gangsta look.

NatBLKMascTop: Not really, but pretty damn close. Fortunately, now that I'm semi-retired I can get away with it a bit more.

PigBoiBottom: Semi-retired?

NatBLKMascTop: Yeah. After roaming around from thing to thing, I was fortunate enough to fall into a lucrative side career a few years back that brandish me the opportunity to break free of the grind…a little bit of it anyway.

PigBoiBottom: Need to find that career. I hate to ask, but what's your age?

NatBLKMascTop: When I got your mouth and ass bouncing between both of my dicks, you can feel free to ask me anything you want. I'm in my late thirties. You?

PigBoiBottom: Twenty-nine. You never did say where you're from.

NatBLKMascTop: East Coast.

PigBoiBottom: Where?

NatBLKMascTop: I'm from…

PigBoiBottom: Oh, I got some friends that just moved out there

NatBLKMascTop: Good place to be. I left some of the best badunkadunks back that way. I wonder how you measure up.

PigBoiBottom: Let me sit on your face and find out.

NatBLKMascTop: You got a smart mouth for somebody that is at my command…and for that…

PigBoiBottom: You slapped an eye mask on my face.

NatBLKMascTop: You damn right. You're no longer PigBoiBottom. You're just a sloppy hole.

PigBoiBottom: Hot.

NatBLKMascTop: Slut.

PigBoiBottom: Damn right.

NatBLKMascTop: I know you are now.

PigBoiBottom: You slapped me!

NatBLKMascTop: I'm sorry.

PigBoiBottom: You're choking me!

NatBLKMascTop: I'm sorry.

PigBoiBottom: What the hell?!?!

NatBLKMascTop: I just busted a nutt down your throat with plenty of icing to spare for that pretty little face of yours. Happy Birthday!

PigBoiBottom: I thought it took you a long time to cum.

NatBLKMascTop: It does. That why my original guy is still pounding out your asshole…in spite of you over there tightening up on that asshole trying to drain my energy. Just like in real life, I got too much stamina for your ass to take me out. PigBoi.

PigBoiBottom: I got stamina too. That's why it took two of you to take me down.

NatBLKMascTop: I never said you didn't. That's why I don't understand if your ass is such a pig why don't you crank that vibrator to full blast! Have it shake like a Polaroid picture.

PigBoiBottom: Is…that good…enough for…you!

NatBLKMascTop: Damn that's the body rock, ain't it? Can you type?

PigBoiBottom: Oh, yeah…but I don't really want to.

NatBLKMascTop: You want to lay down like your friend on the screen and enjoy the ride, don't you?

NatBLKMascTop: Sliding in and out of that juicy badunkadunk.

PigBoiBottom: Yeah.

NatBLKMascTop: You wish there was a real man ramming those walls in.

PigBoiBottom: Yeah.

NatBLKMascTop: Building them up and tearing them down with every hard and powerful stroke.

PigBoiBottom: Yeah.

NatBLKMascTop: Relax. There you go. Just lean back in your chair and let Big Poppa do the rest.

PigBoiBottom: Oh,

NatBLKMascTop: Yeah, bring that ass up a bit more to me, like I was there fucking you in that chair.

PigBoiBottom: Yeah.

NatBLKMascTop: Let me take that ass from a royal warming to piston white-hot.

PigBoiBottom: Oh, yeah. Ohh, yeah!

NatBLKMascTop: I feel that you're holding back on me. Turn that shit up as high as it will go.

PigBoiBottom: Yes sir.

NatBLKMascTop: How does it feel?

PigBoiBottom: Great.

NatBLKMascTop: I see you over there panting. Breathe through it, motherfucker. Don't tell me you've been oinking all these years and you hadn't learned Breathing 101.

PigBoiBottom: Yes sir.

NatBLKMascTop: There you go. Breathe, baby, breathe. Don't be afraid to let your feet rest on that desk.

PigBoiBottom: Ohh,

NatBLKMascTop: Spread that shit like you got your man diving in between them.

PigBoiBottom: Ohh,

NatBLKMascTop: Spread that shit like you were my ho.

PigBoiBottom: Yes sir. I wish you were here sir.

NatBLKMascTop: I am. Just relax your mind and let your body flow from what you feel and what you see on screen.

PigBoiBottom: Yes sir.

NatBLKMascTop: How does it feel?

PigBoiBottom: Like I'm taking care of you, sir.

NatBLKMascTop: Watch how that mouth breathe through each stroke.

PigBoiBottom: I have no choice, sir, my balls are bound to my wrist and if I pull back too tight…

NatBLKMascTop: And here you thought you were in control.

PigBoiBottom: No, sir. You are.

NatBLKMascTop: That's right. When a real man like me is digging you out you got no choice but to take a back seat. Big Poppa got you fully covered.

PigBoiBottom: That's some kick-ass insurance!

NatBLKMascTop: Manners.

PigBoiBottom: Sorry, sir.

NatBLKMascTop: Damn, boy your slick with sweat!

PigBoiBottom: Yes, sir. That's what happens when I got something working out my ass. I wonder if I got a vibrator here and you in me in the computer would that necessarily constitute as being double-teamed?

NatBLKMascTop: Think of it as one in the same. You're watching yourself getting fucked while getting fucked.

PigBoiBottom: Oh, sir, I wish you were really here fucking me! This may sound weird as fuck, but I can feel every stroke. Like way inside me far past this thing can go.

NatBLKMascTop: That was the intention.

PigBoiBottom: You switched scenes?

NatBLKMascTop: Nope. I just got you out of bondage and put you in a chair just like you are just so you can REALLY feel it.

PigBoiBottom: Yes, sir. I want to really feel it sir.

NatBLKMascTop: Do as I said before let your mind become one with the screen. Can you feel it?

PigBoiBottom: Yes, sir. Oh, yes sir.

NatBLKMascTop: You feel this big-ass dick using that sloppy hole?

PigBoiBottom: Yes, sir.

NatBLKMascTop: You hear it talking back?

PigBoiBottom: Oh, sir yes.

NatBLKMascTop: While you're throwing it back?

PigBoiBottom: Yes, sir, yes.

NatBLKMascTop: You hear my balls bouncing against that phat badunkadunk back door of yours?

PigBoiBottom: Oh, God, yes! I hear you making it twerp back. Oh, damn!

NatBLKMascTop: Let it talk to me. Let it say everything you can't.

PigBoiBottom: Oh, yes sir.

NatBLKMascTop: Damn, you're sweating and panting even harder. Brace yourself against the back of your chair with your arm…keep those feet on that desk…there you.

PigBoiBottom: Oh, damn, fuck me.

NatBLKMascTop: You're good at typing with one hand.

PigBoiBottom: Thank you, sir.

NatBLKMascTop: How's that hole feeling?

PigBoiBottom: Raw. Like an all-out gangbang.

NatBLKMascTop: With one man.

PigBoiBottom: Yes, sir. Ohhhhhhhh.

NatBLKMascTop: Are you...

PigBoiBottom: No, sir. Not yet but getting really close.

NatBLKMascTop: Look at that precum just slinging from left to right from your dick.

PigBoiBottom: Yes, sir.

NatBLKMascTop: Look at those legs quivering. Don't push that vibrator out, now. Push that shit all the way back in. If you have to, try your best to lock it in place with your ass cheeks.

PigBoiBottom: Yes, sir...got it.

NatBLKMascTop: Grab your dick and start stroking it. Stroke it to the beat of us fucking on the screen...of the vibrator in your ass, tickling your guts. There you go. There ain't nothing like a quivering hole attached to a cringing man that is about ready to explode.

SHOOT THAT LOAD MOTHERFUCKER! SHOOT IT!

WITH YOUR MOUTH OPEN, MOTHERFUCKER!

TRY TO SHOOT IT UP IN THERE.

YOU LOOK LIKE YOU'RE A GUSHER SHOOTER.

SHOOT IT NOW!

DAMN, THAT LOOKS HOT!

Wow, I was right about your ass! You shot it up in your face. You got some on the corner of your mouth. Lick that shit with your tongue.

There you go.

PigBoiBottom: Wow, sir. That was amazing.

NatBLKMascTop: It ain't over yet I'm still fucking the shit out of you.

PigBoiBottom: Yes, sir. I thought you came inside me after my ass clammed down on it.

NatBLKMascTop: I even work well through pressure.

PigBoiBottom: Yes, sir, you do. I want to take care of you sir. I want to see you cum sir.

NatBLKMascTop: Don't worry about me just yet. Tell me how does your cum tastes in your mouth?

PigBoiBottom: It tastes like pineapple juice, sir.

NatBLKMascTop: It does, huh?

PigBoiBottom: No, sir. I want to taste yours. I don't care if I got to come over there or you come over here. I got to taste it sir.

NatBLKMascTop: Now?

PigBoiBottom: Now, sir. If you still want me and my used hole and cummy mouth?

NatBLKMascTop: Shit, yeah! Who you think made it that way!

YOUNG BUCK

Some guys are just fucks.

Okay, *most* guys are just fucks.

Then, there are some that just look like they might be a really good fuck based on one or more physical attributes. Only a fraction of that, however, turns out to be really good at what they do, be it throwing back a phat ass or honing their sword-swallowing skills suppressing gag reflexes. But what do you say exactly to a young buck that says he feels like a "bitch-ass ho" ass-naked on your bed?

With his ass up, head down, spread legged just kneeing the hell out of a Sealy Posturepedic, looking him in the eye and tell him to "go ahead and feel that way, folk" because he most definitely is. Don't be afraid to tell him so if he probes. He know he is, and deep down he knows he want to be a bitch-ass ho for the right kind of man-meat.

Mine just recently was this neighborhood kid name Alfredo, standing on his usual corner outside of my house clowning on this roly-poly kid that should have been out of his social league. And rather than stoop down to his childish level and call him out on it, I called Alfredo and his sorry-ass over behind my gate.

He was a nineteen-year-old son of a bitch fronting like he was twenty-one, always totting around a double-tall can of malt liquor like it was his adult-size pacifier. Based on pure looks alone, the walnut-colored Honduras-Guatemalan-American hybrid could easily have passed for older if he wanted to. He was a thick solid boy at five-foot-nine with this heavily filled-in strand of a connecting moustache and goatee surrounded by the permanent five o'clock shadow that was otherwise meant to be his beard.

Alfredo was the good kid. The honor roll student. The one she least had to worry about. He was the second oldest of six, and the role model for the other four. His brother was the one that cut class, cut school. His brother was the one that was always the one that got into trouble. Getting suspended or expelled. It was his brother that fell into the wrong crowd, moving up from petty gangbang to hard-time dope-slinger. His brother was the one that started his own cartel and is doing eight consecutive life sentences for murder and other charges in a maximum security prison.

His mother told me their life story in her search of a husband—or at least trying to make me her·man.

Alfredo was rattled by indirect threats he received from his brother's foes his junior year. His brother was his great protector. He made sure that Alfredo made it home every night along with his books and daily lessons. Alfredo was like most inner-city kids, he didn't fear dying. It was a looming part of life with stray bullets almost always equipped with plenty of anonymous names. His greatest fear was getting robbed, because to get robbed in a bad neighborhood, your neighborhood, was to be a marked man from here on out. Unless he had veins of ice or retaliated, his victim status would show every time he walked the filthy streets of fear. It was already had. His brother was making it worst stepping on some toes, peeing on some trees already peed on. Alfredo was hearing from across the way that they were eyeing him to teach his brother a lesson, beating him up or breaking a limb or worst—rape.

He told me about everything except the latter anyway. It was too deplorable for him to mention, fearing that if he spoke of it, it would be a case of *Beetlejuice*. But I kept my ears to the street and know that prison is nothing more grad school for criminals. The way they are putting them in and spitting them out, the cons quickly learn that to humiliate a man to a powdery finest is to take his manhood, turn him out. Flip him over, and make him fiend for blood-throbbing dick like a bitch in heat.

It was enough to scare the shit out of him, making him drop out senior year.

I saw the conflict in his eyes the first time his mom sent him over with a pie for me. He was curious with lust in his eyes, trying not to look too hard. Once glance, however, is all that is needed to give a green egg like him away. Making up some lame excuse to stick nearby, helping me eat some pie and prolong his visit with meaningless conversation.

He tried to gauge me, not as a potential suitor for his mother but someone he hopes will break him in to feed his budding interest. He has two eyes, I'm a good-looking single man rejecting the advance of drop-dead gorgeous women throughout the neighborhood, and judging by the number of births that will easily put out.

Alfredo didn't want to be bitched out. He just wanted a taste on his terms, as sort of way to curve of a possible addiction. If he likes it, he likes it—on the down low. If not, no need to obsess over it. His only problem is that enough to send him on his way with a few jack-off fantasies to last him for a few months. Unaware that the older I get, the less patience I have for young bucks, especially the trouble I have breaking them in. It doesn't matter if they are first-timers or experienced bottom bitches, I already know (not to be braggadocios) that taking my dick is no walk in the park. It took me years to learn that I was working with too much to just ram it in at will. Back when I was young and just tapping some hungry ass I really didn't give a shit if the screams were pleasure or pain as long as I got mine in the end, ignoring every cry to "pull it out" or "it burns" or "it hurts" on and on in between. Nowadays, I can get mine and whoever I'm with can get theirs, too. The downfall of that is that it made me a better more attentive lover. While it shored up the Bootycall Rolodex it can be disastrous event for newbies before unknowingly wising up and becoming jaded to the scene. Starting out naïve in thinking that getting sex in the first few hours of meeting is nothing more than a piece of ass, not an introductory counting ritual. Even worse, the nine out of ten-ers novices like Alfredo that were sure to catch lovesick fever believing that a good fuck-down is the beginning of some grand love story decorated with all the bells and whistles.

He is smart enough to know that to stay close is to stay in mind. So he bides his time by standing out on the corner in front of my abode like a loyal little pup waiting for that "come here boy" call.

He knows better too than to come across eager and hungry for it, setting himself up as a boy to be bitched. He instead created his own little clique from around the way as a diversion. He was too sorry to go the route of his incarcerated brother. He knew that there were booty bandits inside just waiting to drill deep in the valley of his two ripe mounds. Because of his brother and his legacy of going away as a "baaad" motherfucker, he was often courted by the local gang to bring some of his "baaad" blood to the mix. He declined each and every time, keeping his alliance at a distance. He knew if he joined that either a rival gang or his own would kill him for bringing nothing worthwhile to the table. He couldn't go out like no punk, neither. The streets were bound to speak. He secretly envied his peers smart enough to finish school, and go off to school to do their thing. He made his choice he had to do his thing too.

Rather than swim like a big fish in a big pond, Alfredo remained a big fish in a small pond, hanging around younger more impressionable rebels to feed into his ego, instilling in them his philosophies about life and the neighborhood. He knew as long as he stayed in his lane as far as the drug dealers and gangbangers were concerned that he had nothing to worry about, especially if he did some mild recruiting or the side for them. And it didn't hurt that he was standing in front of my house either.

The neighborhood was rough, but carried itself like an unruly family founded by love, with me being scored as the crazy-ass arsenal-owning real "OG" uncle that everybody respected and nobody fucked with. The only father figure of sorts for most of the neighborhood that they love and mild feared.

It was the kind of street cred backup that he needed since he never served a day in his life. I had no doubt that he packed some heat, a piece of steel his big brother probably left behind. Knowing the streets like I do, it was only enough to scare. Otherwise, he was too broke to buy the bullets for it and too scared to fire it off. Yet, it was just what he needed to make his wild, make-up anecdote sound halfway plausible to a group of intoxicate brains in training.

When I called his ass over from behind the fence, it was because I was growing sick and tired of his mouth cracking on his overweight subordinate out there. I figured that if he wanted to play superior, I would take the time and show him who was boss. But by the way he was sporting the biggest, cheesiest Kool-Aid smile I had even seen, he was strutting around like he was due to collect some big cash reward. But the two of us knew what he though he was there to collect. He tried to make himself come off more "willing" by stumbling like he was high on his beer buzz with that "go ahead, take advantage of me, Pa" look.

Never being the one to knowingly take it or getting some while the other was under the influence, I sat his ass down in front of the television, giving his friend plenty of time to make a gracious exit home. My intent was to keep Alfredo around for a sitcom or two, but these steady streams of movies kept coming across the wire. After a few snacks and dinner, it was a little passed midnight. I was ready to send him home when we saw that the gangbangers had stationed themselves in front of his house. Alfredo was cool enough with the gang not to be bothered, but not cool enough to stall through their makeshift camp for the night. So with no choice in my hand, I let him spend the night. (I could've walked him home without incident, but for a nineteen-year-old boy to be walked home by an older man was to suggest he was some kind of pussy boi which would've been the equivalent to getting rob.)

I tried my best to put him out on the sofa in the living room, but he had other ideas. Every fifteen minutes or so, he was barging into my bedroom bugging me about something or other. I forgot how he did, but I ended up conceding letting him sleep in the bed beside me.

The next morning just as the sun was making its way through the burglar-barred window, I find myself humping my hips up in the air with this weird sensation as if I am going to pee. I realize that it wasn't so as I opened my eyes to find his sloppy wet mouth on the end of my pole. If I wasn't so chose to loosing it, I would have slapped him away. Instead the primal beast inside me locked his gagging mouth in place against each hard kick of white juice my body shot out.

I don't bother to ask questions, just catch my breath. I've been told for years now that I sometimes had a tendency to fuck in my sleep. My friends and pieces thought it was a plug for my insatiable appetite. My doctor diagnosed me with the condition.

As I calm down, come to the realization of what happened Alfredo cowered to the side of the bed crying wiping the corners of his mouth. The beast in me wanted him to stew in what he started, let him ask was that what he wanted. The human side however won out, climbing out of the bed to console him.

I apologized. But quickly reminded him I was grown-ass man that do grown-ass things with grown-ass people. And while the law told him he was legal, he wasn't ready to play in the big leagues.

He took my words to heart, or that was what it looked like. He explained himself in a blubbering mess that he saw me getting hard in my sleep. He tried not to give it much thought, he said, but it was there and hard, the biggest he had ever seen outside of poor. Though that didn't say much, seeing that he hadn't had much experience in seeing them outside of the room he shared with his brother. He thought a quick touch would do, satisfy his curiosity. Once he got away with that, he thought he would get his hands around it, but was amazed that his hand could barely fit. He said with the foreskin peeling back and showing off the head and some drool, so he thought he would go in for a taste. One thing led to another, and he was sucking.

It took me along while to realize that he wasn't crying because he got caught or that I held his head down, it was the fact that I came in his mouth that he thought made him a fag. According to hood logic, he was a fag simply for being on the other end of a spitting dick. Being the older wiser man that I am, I tried telling him that he was one long before he put my dick in his mouth. Forget about going through with it, he was thinking about it long before, trying to work his way into my house, into my bed. So, the fact was, there were no hooting and hollering over spilled milk now. The best he could hope for was that the gangs outside didn't find.

The first thing he asked was I going to tell. I assured him that I wasn't and had no reason to. However, seeing that he tried sucking me off in my sleep, he was prone to dick, and to badly paraphrase him 'the bigger the better.' He was his worst enemy on telling on himself, checking out the bulge of every swinging dick that strolled by. Since mine was his first, no major leaguers were safe. He was bound to be wondering around in the streets coping anonymous feels.

He had to be prepared, I told him. He was setting himself up for the gamut. He could be called to perform a duty or get his ass whup. And if word got out that he was a cocksucker that the load I unleashed in his mouth might become the permanent aftertaste of everything else he put into his mouth.

I scared the shit out of him, telling him all this along with the lingering thread I could still beat his ass. He took it all in, wondering what he could do to not to turn into a dick-fiend?

I sheepishly smiled at the reflection in the mirror, giving myself a gentle reminder that I didn't start this, he did. He steeped in the lion's den, and I was ready to feast.

I looked down at his big brown eyes and told him that it was okay if he morphed into a dick fiend, he just needed a steady fix from time to time. I told him until he was certain who was for or against feeding his addition that I might be a good fix for awhile. That didn't mean, however, that he needed to be at my door every waking minute of every freaking day. "Just play it cool like normal, and when I see that you're breaking out into seizures, I'll call you over." His body seemed to relax after that as I made my way back to my feet with my dick hard in his face.

He tried not to seem so eager, but with my blessings he tried to go back to work on it. Because I was mostly sleep through the first part, I took note of his lack of experience. He had the unbridle enthusiasm that most first-timers have, making up for his lack of skill. I tried coaching him through, but he was too caught up in his own to pay me no mind.

How the hell I came the first time baffled me. Alfredo had no skill or finesse. It was just a wet tongue with drool all around the head, ignoring the rest of the shaft and balls. I was beginning to get frustrated, telling him that neither of us was leaving that room until I got off again—even if that meant me being the one to pop his cherry. He seemed to be a bit confused by that as I explained that for me, it meant getting up in his ass.

He tried his best to come up with things just so that wouldn't even happen. In a few instants, he was beginning to master working his mouth just right. But since I had talked myself into getting some ass, his ass I didn't feed into his ego of a job well done. I just told him that I wanted some ass.

Of course, Alfredo tensed up again. It wasn't rocket science that a dick like mine wasn't made to break in virgin like him. I agreed with him, letting him know about my distain for newcomers. I assured his, though, that I was probably the best choice throughout the entire neighborhood, because those gangbangers were three times as sadistic as I was at that age, telling him about my good times in the hood running trains on the lames boys. The gangbangers weren't above that either, fearing that if word got out that Alfredo gave head—pretty decent head—that the gangbangers would probably pimp him out to any and every man hungry for some man-ass on top of sharing him amongst themselves.

He knew that it wasn't passed them since they were always looking for a way to bond their brotherhood and what a better way to do that with money and sex. There was another option I knew about that involved transporting things up his ass. I felt he was still a bit green to know about those things. Plucking away his cherry was a different story.

It took a little coaching but I got him on the bed. Butt-naked, ass up, legs spread and kneeing the bed looking back over at me secretly wonder how he get from rubbing one out in his bed to being put doggy-style on the bed.

I flash him a smirk, answering his burning question: YOU PLAY TOO DAMN MUCH! I was going to let the shit ride. He had other well-thought out plans to get my attention and he did, putting his mouth on a sleeping giant. He thought he was just going to play with it and bounce? No, sir. I thought about sparing his fate for another day. Let him jack off for another day or two. Then, as I looked down, I saw it, centered at the helm of two smooth beautiful brown mounds.

I'm not the one to get excited over an asshole. Many of them are a dime a dozen just like random fucks. This one here was special, and it had absolutely nothing to do with his virgin status. Most fucks who fuck don't understand that to have been in one ass is the same as being in every ass. Every piece of ass is not the same. Like dicks, assholes and tunnels come in different shapes and sizes specially made for different types of equipment. I was feeling a little honored looking at the type of hole he had. In my own lexicon, I called it the universal socket, which is nothing more than a surprising long open slit in oppose to the standard round puckered hole. To the untrained eye it would look like Alfredo takes dick like a pro, the way it opens up on the outside and come together inside at its pale pink lips sort of like a double-entry way.

What makes it most special than the rest is that it is hard to come by, and for a man with a big dick it is quite accommodating being if the man on the other end of it is a virgin or not. His tell-tell sign of never being hit in the ass before is that as a norm if it had been pried open with some dick, it has a tendency to automatically gape open for some more. Regardless, I knew after a few good strokes with him learning how to relax back there, of course, I would be sliding my way in and out of a good time.

As I said, Alfredo was ass out looking back at me telling me that he feels like a "bitch-ass ho." I hadn't the heart to tell that he was just yet. I eased his fears by pulling his dick back between his chunky legs and gently sucked him off. H e was so in nirvana that I don't even think he knew about my wet finger in his ass until it brushed against his prostate. He was telling me that my blowjob was great, but if I kept playing with his prostate he was bound to pee. Knowing that he wasn't, I told him to go ahead. I don't think he heard me though. My tongue was snaking up his undershaft to the long crack that was his hole. I had him panting like a dog. He was practically howling once I got his nipples involved with my fingers.

I guided him over to the nightstand where I kept a hefty supply of magnum condoms and some anal lube that he threw back at me, desperate for me to get back to eating him out. Not one to disappoint, I straight-up tongue-fucked him all the while slipping on the rubber and some lube.

I got behind him, mounting him, rubbing the head of my dick between Opening One and Opening Two before his mouth told his consciousness to fuck him. I play with him a little more before going in for that long deep stroke. He's crying and screaming into his pillow, telling me that I'm splitting him in two I told him to relax. Try to relax, get into it. And like magic my dick stretched and plunging his hole to the point I had every inch buried to the nuts. Alfredo seemed to be getting off on that, the sound of this rhythmic beat.

He was getting into it, and so was I, forgetting that this was his first time out. He was so caught up I had to remind his to breath. We were both sweating hard about fifty minutes into it. I could've gone much longer but had to remind myself once against he was still a newbie. The way we were going at it he was bound to be sore for the next couple of days. So I held him tight and filled the condom inside of him.

I pulled out. Tossing the evidence in a nearby trashcan and rolled on my back, taking the time to catch my breath. I guess Alfredo took the cue for that to mean for him to lay on top of me. Rather than that, I told him to round up and get his ass home. It wasn't that I was trying to be cruel; I just wasn't going to let him believe that it was something more that what it was—a good fuck.

EXIT INTERVIEW

with Diesel King
by R. Talent

Who is Diesel King?

Diesel King is an alter ego of mine for the last past twenty-some-odd years. Unlike the real me that is apprehensive about disclosing my criminal record and sexual past upon initial meeting, my alter ego will put everything out there on Front Street and will pimp out every filthy detail—the good, the bad, and the downright ugly.

Who is Bossman?

My go between my everyday self and Diesel King. Regardless of who I have to be in the moment, I strive to be the very best, which in black slang means the very best of everything or the leader or a leader.

So you are black?

What gave that away? (*Laughs.*) One hundred and ten percent. Three-fourths African-American and one-fourth black Latino. My granddaddy was one part Cuban and one part Dominican but he was born and bred in Puerto Rico.

If your grandfather was half as handsome as you are, I take it that you have family scattered across the Caribbean?

It's sort of a family tradition, so to speak. He was a strikingly handsome, in his youth and old age. He was a well-educated, well-traveled musician that was great with his hands and had a heavy but romantic accent that made women of all ages knees buckle.

I don't care about the women. I only care about those people with those dingalings.

He buckled a few knees with the men, too. It was never openly talked about back then, or ever, but he did have a few boyfriends back in the day. As he got older, he got sloppier with his affairs, with both men and women, I mean. I never will forget the day I caught one of his musical tutees coming out of his apartment with that horrified look, wiping his mouth and face trying to get rid of that slimy white stuff, if you know what I mean.

Oh, damn. Go 'head grand-pa! So he wouldn't be mean-mugged too badly about what you do, if he knew what his beloved grandson did in the bedroom? Does he?

The only thing he would mean-mug me about would be about me waiting so damn long to father children. By the time he was the age I am now, he was working on great grandchildren while still working on children and grandchildren. He started out very young—family tradition. (*Laughs.*)

What's so funny?

How he found out about me. (*Laughs.*)

Do tell.

Back when I was younger and living on the west coast the first time, I used to travel across the board to have a little fun. Unbeknownst to either one of us, both of us were down in Tijuana graciously being treated to the "hospitality" of a popular male brothel down there when we emerged out of our respective holes with our tricks. Normally, I'm not a man that is easily embarrassed— shy sometimes, but never embarrassed. But on this rare occasion, I was mortified. I mean I knew or suspected he messed around because of what I said earlier, but I was being called on my stuff, too. I wanted to go run and hid somewhere, not really taking into account in the moment that we were both in the same place. My granddaddy, on the other hand, was bold. He looked square in my eyes from across the hall as he threw in an extra tip to his manwhore, and told me roughly in Spanish that "bitches get pregnant, fags don't" and walked it off like it was nothing!

Habla español?

No…well, muy pequeño. I can understand it far better than I can speak it or read it. I know some the basics when it comes to reading. He was huge about assimilating when he came over here from Puerto Rico and thought it was beneath his descendents to learn Spanish until it became sort of cool.

Let's get back to business at hand. Was this your first writing adventure?

No. I have been published in a few anthology collections here and there, under my real name and my other pseudonyms, including this one, for years. It is however my first time taking on a project of this magnitude on my own.

How was it?

Bittersweet. It was a lot more difficult than I thought, but rewarding and reminiscent. It would seem that one would natural assume that since you lived this stuff that it would be a piece of cake to write. Some stuff was. Others—because it was so real—was harder to pen down because I had to draw from pure memory along with giving the reader a nice little descript of the people and places I was describing, and always second and third guessing if the reader would get it however it is put down. Then, too, I had to make sure that I protected the guilty by changing their names! I got to admit it got confusing at times when I was in the thick of writing it down.

What made you decide to? Decide to pen an anthology, I mean?

Getting older. Wanting to write the great American cum towel. Yadda. Yadda. Yadda.

What really put the fire under my butt was this erotic story I came across a few years back. It wasn't the best story ever written, but it kept me reaching for my dick on those cold lonely nights and had me busting nutts like it was my first time because it had a decent plot.

You figured if he can do it you can too?

Yeah. It was just right there in front of me.

How so?

Before I went "Hollywood", so to speak, as they call coming up where I am from, or ever could afford to jet set to a place its equal in stature, it was the only place I could have a good time was in the hood. My hood, whatever hood was in at the time.

So that's what you started to write about?

Not exactly. Not because I didn't want to but because I got schooled in this writing biz real quick.

Keep in mind that way back when most publishing companies that distributed gay erotica didn't want to publish black writers, or rather black stories featuring all-black characters, crying that it wouldn't be profitable. I hooted and hollered, of course, to each and everyone one of them that I could get a hold of. After enduring rejection after rejection, I went on my usual rant to more publishers and editors until I came across one that genuinely and sincerely agreed with me. He was an older white guy, and he told me that he and many of his white friends felt the same exact way. The need for diversity in erotic, especially as it relates to black men. He told me it could be done and be profitable. But the thing he feared was that his higher ups would try to make it more of a Mandingo fantasy for its white readers than just a story to be apart of the fold. He suggested that in order to make my characters more digestible to editors that I start making my stories interracial.

But wasn't—

Exactly. And before I could go there, he immediately injected that I just write the story well, and that the characters simply be. Like, my characters could be such-and-such he was such-and-such because of the type of man he was, not because of the color of his skin or the size dick or the plumpness of his ass.

Did it work?

It did. Unfortunately, it worked a little too well because now everybody expected interracial interlude when I wrote under that pseudonym. That was fine. However, my real life interracial action was more on the line of black and Latino or black and Asian, Middle Eastern, South American, Native American, whatever, more so than black and white, because nine times out of ten, if I was going to hook up with a white boy I had to go where the white boy hung out. This wasn't so much a problem as it was a hindrance to my writing. I would or could, pretty much, meet these guys at a bar or a club or a sex party or a bathhouse or a truck stop or rest stop, whatever.

So the culture in which things were going be done was already set?

Exactly. You already know going into these places or certain places what is bound to transpire, which is sex. That's the whole reason why your there. That was the driving force behind going in the first place.

No surprise.

You hit it right on the nose…with the exception that maybe elsewhere you was fortunate enough to come across a white boy in the world that had no shame whatsoever about what he does and what he wants you to do to him. There was this one time where I was working on a construction site and around lunch time—

Let me stop. Where was I? No surprises. And because I was a huge black guy jacking a nice piece, I always had to wean through the most of these places to get what I sought out. Pretty much, usual being the "token" black guy in these places, there was always those that didn't want "my kind" around or saw MANDINGO plastered across my broad chest just so I could get to the kind of man that I liked—a hot one.

In other words, interracial is the way to go? But—

Not exactly. It made my writing more digestible to many of the naysayers without them even knowing it. Even to the point of complimenting me about putting "meat" in my stories without just injecting the cliché sensational words like *dick, ass, hard, fast,* and *cum* just to garner some attention.

Ironically, by going the interracial route I found where the problem laid, of why it was so hard to get black stories published in some of these [publishing] houses. While it is true that there some gay press stand by the creed that "white is the only right" in gay publishing, through some of my emerging contacts, it was brought to my attention that many of these companies weren't really articulating the essence of the real problem.

What is or was the problem?

In a nutshell, black gay men aren't or weren't writing about black men. I hate to say it but it is true. I don't know if it has a lot to do with trying not to play into the stereotype that black men are nothing more than a big dick or what, but many of these stories out there are written by feminine men that I don't know or are not aware or either simply don't care that they are writing stories that are emasculating their characters. So much so it probably would place better in lesbian erotica than gay male erotica.

Ha!

Seriously, I am not trying to be funny. Most gay men of all shade of the rainbow want men, real men in their stories. They want to sense his presence, be it the slim guy to the muscled dad to the hairy furball, whatever. They don't want a question mark over their lead character's head of whether he is or isn't a man, particularly if he is supposed to a black man. Whether either of us likes it or not, black men are sort of looked at as the ultimate standard of masculinity in society. So, if something is suppose to be pure masculine and pure sex and that is your flavor, of course your dick is going to die like the night Chicago died if is cloaking a bitch in heat underneath! You want a man—100% pure and unadulterated.

Look at our porn nowadays! If I see one more skinny, twinkish looking wannabe thug squeamish like a little cunt I am going to scream my fucking head off! It said thug not thuggetts with strap-ons. I love tapping into a dude's inner bitch. I love bringing it out of him, especially if he didn't even know it was in him like that. But if that is all that is there then there was no man there to begin with, before or after he takes off his clothes.

I don't need muscles 24/7, but please give me a man no matter what position he plays and make sure it is not an act. If so, make sure he *can* act, *at least*. I don't know which is worse watching a so-called man release his inner "gurl" while getting his back blown out or get one that looks bored as fuck with a gangbang sprouting out of his lame ass!

I see you're passionate about this.

I am. I am a firm believer to each it's own, but when it hurts more than it helps, it gets to me.

Especially when it puts off the dick, I feel that one-hundred and ten percent.

You're on it today, aincha boy? But getting back to what I was trying to say earlier, because there was no median between sex in sex establishments and the hot mess that pass for black gay erotica, I came up with the concept of doing this anthology from what I lived and experience. I am not saying that I am the best that ever done it, the Second Coming or anything like that (though I hope that one of these stories milk a good one out of you). But I would like to think that I am bring black masculinity back to black gay erotica, along with that an intelligence to it.

I think I sort of got an idea where you're going with this. This isn't my interview so you have to explain that.

I don't really have a problem with being a fantasy to most other guys because of my race or my build or my dick size, sometimes all three. Everyday somebody somewhere fantasize about somebody else about something that has absolutely nothing to do with their personality or "inner beauty". Men by nature are visual people, so why hate if our lust drags us by the visual collar. The problem that I have with most people, especially those that are not of my race, is that they want to get screwed by the big black guy with the big black dick because they are ignorant to believe that the reason I got a big dick is to compensate for some lack of intelligence. Not so. Not here at least. I can't speak for every big black man packing a nice jimmie, but there is a function brain above this one, and I do a whole lot more thinking with the bigger head than I do with the big one. And while the doors are slightly ajar for other black gay erotic writers to enter nowadays, I think with everybody trying to jump on this homo thug wagon, that while entertaining, the intelligent side might not shine through.

How is that?

One concern is pure sex with no plot in the world of erotica. I mean, it can be cool sometimes but I thought what separated erotica from porn was that it contained some kind of poetic element to it that didn't always lead to skeeting a nutt. It should most times, but sometimes it just is. My most pressing concern with other black writers is language. I may not can speak or write in perfect English, but there is very little doubt to anyone around that it is my given language.

Now, I'm hood. Born and bred. I never had the privilege of being part of the boogie aspect of my community. So why is it that I was born and raised in the hood and never heard or seen some of the stuff spewed on these pages? I mean, I grew up with slang and code and heavy accents. I will even give you those that are terrible at pronouncing things, but when you have to let your eyes rest like one of those 3-D pictures to make out what is being said, Houston we have a fucking fucked-up problem! I really don't differentiate between American English and Ebonics because neither falls into the parameters of proper English, so to speak. But dude, c'mon! What's the point of writing a story that nobody understand? Even those that you consider apart of your audience or whom you are trying to represent?

I feel you. You feel like nobody is representing your side of town without making all of you looking like no talkin' buffoons.

Exactly. I remember at time when a brotha went to jail and came out talking like he earned his PhD. Nowadays, some of these kats come out dumber than the day they went in. And while I get you're trying to put an authenticity to our voices. Don't do so where it gives off the wrong impression? I think there is a way to strike a balance to represent and keep it real. Iceberg Slim, Chester Himes, or Donald Goines did it, why can't we?

Are those are some of your influences?

Yeah, a few of them, I like the old and the new especially when it offers street intelligence with some grit and grime, you know?

You look youthful but have this refinement that you've somehow been around the block a few times. How old are you?

You want the truth or the PC answer?

I'm a risk-taker. I want the PC answer and then the truth.

The PC answer is that I am old enough for your young ass to call me Daddy and love it. You may not like it, but dammit you will love it! (*Laughs.*)

Truth?

Old enough to be called a pervert by dating an 18-year-old buck, but young enough to still look good doing it.

I can see that. You got that swagger about you. What is your sexual preference? I remember you saying mentioning having a kid earlier.

Kids. By label standards I would either be called bisexual or pansexual. I hate labels. I just loving making my dick spit and having a satisfied being on the other end while I do so.

Alright. I ain't mad. So are you a top? Bottom? Vers? Oral?

(*Laughs.*) I find it funny you even have to ask. (*Wink.*)

You never know nowadays.

True that. But it is usually to my benefit, though. (*Laughs.*) I am a top. I am not one of those tops that will tell you that I never been fucked before or ate out or anything like that. Though I got a very late start, I can pretty much count on two hands all the times I've bottom over my two scores plus. It was what it was, and now my dick chooses.

Big Poppa's over forty, huh? Cool. Not a good experience?

Unlike most people, my first time getting fucked was very enjoyable. Which threw me for a loop because in all the years I was fucking it was never anything I really wanted to pursue. Thinking back on my first time now, it is kind of scary that my ass was able to swallow up two of those one-eyed monsters like that. Those fucking bastards were packing some mad mutant dick. I'm talking about the kind of fuckers that no first-timers had any business looking at much less starting off on. The kind that most professional-grade fudge packers wouldn't even dare mess with. Don't get it twisted, it hurt at first, but after the three of us found this wicked groove, we were fucking golden. You hear me? I talked about the experience in this anthology.

If the dicks were that good, why give up the ghost? Why become a total top?

I don't think ever I *became* a total top. I always was, by nature. That's probably why it took me all the way to my mid-thirties to even try bottoming, twenty years after I first began fucking. Let me explain.

I got this cool-ass rough-and-tumble white boy that is a frequent fuck buddy of mine that sort of put it in prospective. He'll tell you that he's a total bottom. And he's one of those that though he doesn't act like it he loves having a big dick in his hole just wearing the shit out of it. He said if he could find one of those gynecologist's tables with those foot things, man, he would sleep like that butt-naked ready to take care of a big dick at a moment's notice. But because of his black-man-trapped-in-a-white-boy-body's demeanor, in order to get the dick he fiends for sometimes he has to give up his. So once he met me and saw that all I wanted was some ass and nothing but the ass, and had the piece, the drive, and the stamina to keep him satisfied, he was not only online checking for that table but he was trying to find a spot so we could go ahead and get that marriage certificate.

So, for me, after getting my cherry popped and some of the subsequent sex that followed between me and those two guys, anytime between and thereafter, with anybody else, I felt this almost fiendish need for my dick to be wrapped in something like I did before, if not stronger. It was like I bottomed. I did that. Now can I go on with the rest of the show, you know what I mean?

Yeah. Been there, done that.

Yeah. I should've thrown in the towel the second after the first experience came to ahead because everything else was a waste of sexual energy. But, of course, that's hindsight and different people and places and times in your life make you reconsider some of your so-called hard stances. But it took that for me to finally come to the brilliant conclusion that it just wasn't my thing after I paid attention and listened to the genuine love that most of pieces had for getting dick. It was the same way I felt about getting ass! If there was warm hole readily waiting every time my dick thought about getting hard, I would never leave the house. That is unless I could get it while doing other day-to-day things like driving, get it under my desk at work, when I go to the bathroom, and any other situation you could think of.

The only difference between me and my piece is that our ratios are off. He maybe a total bottom, but most have to throw some dick to get some dick. Whereas I can pretty much snap my fingers and have some ass presented to me just like that with no reciprocation. I'm just a top that experimented. Shoot me!

No need. Sex is an exploration. Now that you've found your niche, I know you loving those boys that know theirs...on the other end of that sweet dick?

Oh, I do. You don't know the half, bruh man! It is a supply that I hope never dries up!

What kind of men do you like?

I love muscle. I can't even lie if I tried. It's just something about them that says that "I'm built to fuck rough." However, I a huge fan of men with those solid, sturdy stocky builds, 100% natural man. Look, even though I'm muscled up myself, I don't care if he got a fat stomach, a beer belly, a six-pack, eight-pack. It really doesn't matter. My main concern is that he is a man first that has a strong masculine element written to him. And I'm good. Great even. Right now, in my life, I just love a man that *thought* he was an alpha male all these years and I have to knock him down to his rightful place as a beta and below.

You said right now. So what changed? What was there before?

When I was a young buck I felt that any ass I could get belonged to a man I liked. As I started coming into my sexuality openly, I was feverishly in lust with feminine guys and she-males. And it wasn't because they were feminine to my masculine like with some guys, as much as there wasn't a song and dance to get them to work on the dick. I'm not saying that they were easy—though some of them were. They just knew that they liked dick and made it their sole mission to take care of mine to the best of their abilities. Anytime, anyplace, and every which way they could get it and they treated me like a king as their appreciation for it. I was always partial to masculine men, even then. Though finding one that was openly willing to bottom was a lot harder to come by back in the day as it is now. So when the masculine bottom started surfacing and were just as eager as their feminine counterparts, I felt like I ascended to the promise land.

Don't get me wrong, though. While I am a bit partial to one end of the gay spectrum than the other, I have a firm rule of not ruling anybody out. I learned a long time ago that what you want and what you need are sometimes two entirely different things, and that everyone has a different way of surprising you.

How big is your dick?

(*Stands up, unzips pants, and cup flaccid penis.*) This big…eleven and seven-eighths of an inch by eight and two-fifths rounds of bubbling brown sugar dick when hard…and it doesn't have a problem saluting like a soldier like some of your porn stars that are packing this kind of meat. Now, I could be technical in giving my measurement each and every time people ask, but I found that telling people that I got twelve-inches of uncut tubesteak is quite a conversation piece amongst friends. Don't you agree?

Damn! Damn! Damn! Damn! Damn!!!

I know…and as you can see it's obviously long *and* thick when soft.

And you got some big-ass low-hangers! It looks like I found those two meatballs that were missing from my sandwich earlier.

Glad you like it.

Okay. Where was I? All of that on one man don't make a bit of sense! Give some of that shit to charity!

And your question?

I'm trying to get my thoughts together. Wait a minute. Damn!

Take your time. (*Zips it back up and sits back down.*)

I hope you do with that thing.

I do. It ain't like I can just ram it in somebody without having to call an ambulance afterwards. I have. But the older you get the more you take into account that it's quite embarrassing for your bottom to tell their doctor and nurse how they ended up there with a bleeding butthole. Hospital bills are no joke, and from what I heard they charge extra for having to deal with a shitty mess. I would've learned my lesson years ago if somebody had sued me for hospital bills. But again, it isn't like they anybody in their right mind was going to sue or press charges without humiliating themselves even further by disclosing everything. Above all else, they don't have a policy of ever returning again to give me another crack at it. Second and third times are always the charm.

I noticed that "cock" was a word you didn't use often, if at all, why is that? If it was intentional?

For the oddest reason, my mind snaps back to old episodes of *Good Times* when Michael played by Ralph Carter was infamous in telling his project family that "boy" is a white racist word. For me "cock" is a rooster, not a body part.

Look, the truth of the matter is that anybody who grew up in black areas knows that unlike in white areas or white diction the word *cock* was rarely used to describe male genitalia, if at all. For the most part, if you're as old as me, the word *cock* in predominately black vernacular was used to describe the female genitalia or even the clitoris as it seems to "cock" out when it is in heat.

We might say, 'she's got a cock on her.' I might say that 'I got a cock opener for her' or say 'she's blessed me with a nice shot of cock in spite of that cock block earlier.'

A man is a cock hound or has a cock opener but not a cock, the way I was raised.

Yet, ironically, over the years, I have grown use to terms like *cockring, cock tease*, or *cocksucker* but cock on a man is just uncivilized.

What is your biggest pet peeve?

Anybody calling a piece of ass *boi pussy, round pussy*, or *pussy* of any freaking kind is my biggest pet peeve. What the fuck?! Ass and pussy have two entirely different grips to them. If you want pussy, snip off your dick and have a pussy surgically implanted! (Laughs.)

Naw, really. Even though it is my biggest pet peeve I won't go off about it or anything like that. I know some dudes that value their boi pussy very much. So as long as it is wet and tight and he knows how to throw it back, I'm good. He can call it a garbage disposal for all I care because I will treat it like a cumdump.

What is your sexual handle, or significant sexual move or turn on?

For me, it is satisfying the other person. I know it sounds kind of cliché, but I get off on being the gatekeeper and host through their sexual exploration. Not to toot my own horn, but I always seem to get some sort of satisfying accolade after the fact. After that, because it takes me forever to cum, I would say bellowing out a nice thick load.

If you're asking what is my signature move, or notoriety, I would have though it was going long and strong with this big fat piggish dick. As of late I've been told by both men and women like is my ability to take the lead in sexual control.

I ain't the kind to get dick-struck but with that between your legs you can lead me anywhere.

(*Laughs*.) I try. I know that having a big dick can get me through a lot of doors when soft. However, I know from talking to people over the years not everybody that has a big dick knows how to use it effectively.

So true. That isn't the case with you though?

Hell, no. But that in large part is because I know my dick is this big and the average asshole isn't just going to magically flare open and take me comfortably without some serious foreplay…especially if I want a standing invitation to hit it again.

That is what I'm talking about!

Babe, I feel that asshole dripping wet from over here!

It's twitching a bit. What is something that you always wanted to do but haven't?

I pretty much got everything that I wanted to do out of my system. Wait a minute, there is one more thing I would like to do again. When I was younger, I ordered me one of those jellied pink pussy masturbators with the opened end. One day after I had these tendencies to stop short of that "dying feeling" and came slowly afterwards, I just grew the balls and just went for the gusto one day, in spite of the feeling that I might loose my life to that fast-approaching orgasm. I literally shot a load that tickled the nine-foot ceiling in my bedroom with a backsplash of cum that was a cleaning to remember. I remembered since dried spunk has a nasty way of leaving hollow spots on dark hardwood floor after awhile.

While I might never be able to milk cream like that ever again, I always wanted to cum by the gallons. I don't do too bad busting a nutt. But I always had this morbid fantasy of spewing enough potent sperm that it nearly clogs a person's throat.

Interesting. What is one quirk about you that most people would find odd? Other than that?

I love to hear moaning and groaning and a bed squeaking to the rhythm. It's sort of like a pacifier to me. But I hate—truly hate—talking during sex, even the dirty kind. I don't mind a few phrases sprinkled here and there to let me know that you're still in the game, especially if you're sincere. I just don't want a Gabby Gab in the bedroom. The same goes for my porn. Weird, I know.

What is one thing you hate in porn?

I sort of touched on it earlier. I can deal with the skinny anorexics, particularly if they can take or ride dick. I can't stand a closed-mouth motherfucker with no sound coming out. It leads me to believe that having a dick up your ass is like something as effortless as breathing. And if you can do it like that, being on the other end of my dick, tells me that you're a dick-stuffed slut with no walls—and not in a good way.

Is porn in your future?

Everyday—oh, in being in one? I have done a few clips for a few sites. As for doing it professionally, I don't know. I've thought about it more since I've gotten older. I make a very comfortable living and built a nice retirement without worrying about it hindering any possible or future career, at this point. I am sort of a part-time playboy now. I guess I would say that if my 50s promises to be as kind to me as my 40s have been so far, I can absolutely see myself doing porn professionally. The question becomes, who would be man enough to allow their hole to get stretched by my dick for the world to see?

What is the weirdest place you ever had sex?

In a coffin in a church on a dare—don't worry everybody was living.

What is the weirdest sex you had?

It wasn't so much as weird as it was awkward. I was down in Brazil where I was in line with about six to seven hundred men getting down with about forty-five to fifty bottoms. Now I am an exhibitionist that loves public sex. The more I have to show off and compete is when I bring my Triple A game. However, the way they had given us so much time to fuck and dispose of our loads in a trashcan made the sex more mechanical than the fun that I knew it should have been—especially for Brazil. Nevertheless, it was an experience. Especially seeing those large trashcans filled to the brim with condoms and cum.

How did you get into kink?

As hard as it maybe to believe, I didn't start out with a sadistic flair. I was dragged every step of the way. Let me stop. Let me correct that.

I was always into kink. I just didn't know I was into kink when I was into kink per se, if that makes any sense? Not in the beginning, at least. It was all about sex and the power it came with it being black and masculine where I grew up, a glowing aphrodisiac in my community.

But I have to say my first intro into kink, or kink as I officially knew it when I knew what it was, I would say it started when I was twenty-two. I had met this Cuban dude whose asshole was so tight that it was locked like Fort

Knox. I mean, bump my dick! I knew I didn't have the key to every door, but I was surprised dude could even shit the way it tried to take off the tip of my finger! That was how tight his hole was. In spite of this, he seemed more fascinated by my black work boots I had on. Not me as a person or my dick or my masculine appeal, but my boots! It took me a minute to get it, but apparently I was competing with my raggedy boots. Once he started licking them, he let me fuck him with joyful abandon. It was like his asshole heard "Open Sesame" and obeyed. I fucked. He munched on my boots. After I came, I headed off the bathroom for a post-nutt piss, which he held my dick while I did it.

A couple of months later, the same dude called me over to his extended stay to suck me off. Unlike most folks who claim they can make a man nutt with one his mouth, he was one of those rare men that were true to his word with no hands. At that point, there was only one person in my life that ever made me come in their mouth without jacking me off first. I tried to pull away but he wouldn't let me. So I came in his mouth, and he swallowed it proudly it like it was some sort of delicious protein shake. So afterwards I headed to the bathroom, but he snake around me and take a seat on the toilet.

I'm thinking by this time that this boy is either slow or messed up, seeing that he see that I am trying to piss. But he informs me that he wants to be the recipient of my piss. I'm not cool with someone standing next to me when I take a piss, but I make due. This dude was telling me to take a piss on him. I wanted to tell him no. Then I thought about it, he ain't trying to do it me. He wanted me to do it to him. No reciprocation. So I piss on his slightly hairy chest and watch it trickle down his protruding belly, I swear with two good hard stroke with my piss as his lube, he came like a bellowing ogre which stopped my dick from going down at all!

So he sucked me off again. But instead of swallowing my load, he made the suggestion that I nutt on my boots. My boots wasn't some sort of cum wipe, so I wasn't fond of the idea until he promised me that he would lick up every drop of cum. Just to see if he would do it, I let loose on them.

Not only did he lick my cum clean off of my boots, he licked both of my boots from top to sole, and then forced me to share a fifth of gin with him so that I could cover his face and head with another long solid arc of alcoholic piss. While piss or bootlicking are no way my thing, never being on the other end of watersports or bootlicking, I quickly found out after that experience that some people can't get their sexual fix without these vices.

Fetishes. Something that was more laughable to me that it was anything serious, or so I thought. But it wasn't until after my trip back to NYC that I saw a man catch the piss of several or so men in his mouth *and* swallowing it while another gang of men (including me) pissed on his body like they were putting out an inferno did I start studying the art of kink and all it had to offer.

Well, that's it! Thank you for your time, Big Poppa.

No, thank you. And if you're interested in doing a face-to-crotch interview with my masterpiece a little later feel free to set up an appointment.

Is right now good?

Of course...but only if I can get a nice helping of that sweet phat badonkadunk of yours. If I got a future in porn, I need to get in as much practice as I can get.

ABOUT THE AUTHOR

Diesel King is the alter ego of a strikingly handsome muscled man of leather and of color, tapping his solid mahogany desk with his thick digits currently penning his first novel.

He has no prior claim to fame other than being a jack-of-all-trades and the insatiable sex machine in between. He is heavily in demand in the cuckold and orgy scenes, and is an all-around sadistic freak oblivious to sexual orientations. He is however partial to his man-sex in the tried and steadily true belief that "most boys will what most girls won't" having plenty of uncut meat to share with the masses.

He once was a drifter mostly confined to the grit and grime of the North American slums before lucking up in a career as a highly in-demand international playboy and poker player. Flanked by this new life, he can be currently found somewhere in the darkrooms of Europe, the secret clubs and societies of Africa, or underground baths of Asia. If not back in some dilapidated neighborhood seeing what new and freaky things he can get into.

6280697R0

Made in the USA
Lexington, KY
05 August 2010